FEB - 2015

FEB 2 5 2021'

DATE DUE

AUG 1 1 '75			
SEP 1 7 75			

Stock-Car Racer

BOOKS BY W. E. BUTTERWORTH

FAST GREEN CAR
RETURN TO RACING
CRAZY TO RACE
RETURN TO DAYTONA
DATELINE: TALLADEGA
FAST AND SMART
YANKEE DRIVER
STOCK CAR RACER
ROAD RACER
MARTY AND THE MICRO-MIDGETS
REDLINE 7100

By *W. E. Butterworth*

STOCK-CAR RACER

GROSSET & DUNLAP
PUBLISHERS • NEW YORK

One

You had to know a little something about cars to be able to tell that Dave Wade's 1959 Studebaker wasn't just a well-cared-for, well-shined, two-door from South Bend.

It looked, to the casual eye, very much the same as all 1959 Studebakers had looked on the showroom floor. As it rolled down Marshall Street and stopped for the stop sign before turning left onto Wilson Avenue, it made no unusual noises. And as Dave went up through the gears again, it made no more noise than any other well-cared-for, six-year-old automobile.

It had only two headlights. There were no spotlights. The radio antenna sat on the left, front fender, where the designers of the 1959 Studebaker had put the antenna. There were no fringes around the windows, no foam dice hanging from the rear-view mirror, and no supposedly witty little signs anywhere on it informing readers that it had been "Made in The Black Forest By Elves" or "Made in Detroit by Idiots." It was the sort of automobile that looked as though it had been driven back and forth to church by a little old lady from Pasadena and kept in the garage the other six days of the week.

But if you looked close as it went past you, you could see certain subtle little differences. From the rear, you could tell that it had one more exhaust pipe than Studebaker had furnished that year. The exhaust was gentle. It hinted at power, but these mufflers had not been gutted so they would make noise.

On each side of the coupe, if you looked close, you could see another set of exhaust pipes. The openings on these were closed neatly with chrome-plated plugs. They were connected to the exhaust manifold of the engine, without mufflers. A lever-and-cable arrangment ending under the dash permitted Dave Wade to direct the engine's exhaust either through the muffler system as it was now or directly to the Hollywood pipes.

Dave pulled into a parking place and shut the engine down. When he pulled the lever, revved the engine, and let the exhaust go through the straight pipes, people within half-a-mile began to scan the sky in search of the low flying airplane.

But he was in the city, and he didn't like to call attention to himself. Dave depressed the pedal that disengaged the weighted, balanced, Holley clutch and, finally, put the Hurst shifting mechanism into its proper place. This put the Borg-Warner, four-speed transmission in neutral. He shut off the key, and these things happened: the transistorized ignition system no longer fed ignition current to the eight Lodge platinum-plated spark-plugs; and the Bendix electric fuel pump stopped delivering a precisely measured amount of fuel to the two Holley four-barrel carburetors sitting on top of the Offenhauser intake manifold, which had replaced the stock Cadillac intake manifold on the Cadillac engine, which had replaced the 1959 Studebaker engine.

When all this happened, the Stewart-Warner tachometer on the dash unwound and pointed to 0 revolutions per minute. When he pulled the parking brake on, took the keys from the ignition, got out and walked around the car, he saw that the 7:10 by 15 Michelin-X tires were three inches from the curb. Satisfied, he walked into the building, and, deciding not to wait for the elevator, went up the stairs two at a time.

The shiny Studebaker was not, in fact, what it looked to be. It had once passed through a precisely measured mile, going first against the wind, and then with it, for an average measured mile speed of 139.582. Around the track and around the more knowledgeable garages, it was said that Dave Wade drove a '59 Stud-illac, with a Borg-Warner four-speed, and an Offy-Holley carb system.

It should have made him happy, for Dave loved fine automotive machinery. Normally it did but today he had a major problem, and very little could have made him feel happy.

At twenty, in the vacation period between his sophomore and junior years at college, Dave stood an inch shy of six feet, and weighed 160 pounds. He was neither small nor large, thin nor fat, muscular nor puny. He was average.

No one likes to be average. The only nice thing that Dave knew about his appearance was that if he finished college and went on to law school, got admitted to the bar, and applied for a position in the FBI, this would be in his favor. The FBI liked its agents to look like everybody else. But, since he was planning to be an engineer, and not to join the FBI, this wasn't the sort of thing that could give a fellow a swelled head.

At the moment, he felt that the opposite was true. He was the original pinhead. He had been so sure that he had been so smart, and now the facts were that he was responsible for the predicament he was in. There was no one else to blame.

Near the end of the corridor on the second floor, he pushed open a frosted glass door on which was written O'HARA AND RUSH, ATTORNEYS AT LAW. The door opened into an anteroom holding several couches and chairs, a table with magazines, several floor type ashtrays, and the desk of Miss Harriet Douglass.

"Hello, Dave," she said, when she saw him. "How are you?"

"Hello, Miss Douglass," he said. "Just fine, thank you."

"You don't look it," she said, with the knowledge of a maiden lady in her sixties who had watched both Dave and Dave's father grow up. "You look as if you ate something that doesn't agree with you."

"No, Ma'am," he said. "Can I see him, do you think?"

"If you're referring to your stepfather, Mr. O'Hara," she said, correcting his manners as she answered, "he's in library. I'm sure he would be glad to see you."

"Thank you," Dave said, and went through an inner door and down an interior corridor until he came to an open door through which he could see his stepfather slumped in an upholstered chair, glasses on the edge of his nose, a thick law book on his lap.

Dave had known Peter O'Hara all his life. Peter O'Hara and Dave's father had gone to high school together, and then been roommates at college. When First Lieutenant David Wade, Army Air Corps, had married a girl he'd met in Marianna, Florida, in 1943, First Lieutenant Peter O'Hara, Infantry, had come down from Fort Benning to be best man.

When David Wade, Junior, had been christened, in 1946, Peter O'Hara had taken time off from law school to participate in the ceremony as godfather. Peter O'Hara and David Wade, Senior, went off to the Korean War together, and when somebody had to tell little Dave that his father wouldn't be coming home any more, Captain Peter O'Hara, late of the fortieth Division, got special permission to leave Walter Reed Hospital, where he was recuperating from his wounds, to perform that unpleasant duty.

It had seemed perfectly fitting and proper that "Uncle" Pete should become an official family member, Dave's mother's husband, two years after that, for he had always been there.

"Hi," Pete said. "Come on in."

"Am I interrupting anything important?"

"If you were, Miss Douglass wouldn't have let you in,"

Peter O'Hara said. "How about a cup of coffee? Maybe it will wake me up."

"Thank you," Dave said. "Stay there. I'll get it."

He went into an anteroom and poured two cups from a pot, putting sugar in his and leaving his stepfather's black.

"How did the accident affect Motor Enterprises?" Peter O'Hara asked, after he had taken a sip of the coffee and nodded his head and smiled his thanks.

"I am now the sole proprietor of Motor Enterprises," Dave replied. "That's what I came to talk to you about."

Peter O'Hara shrugged his shoulders as he digested this information, and then he nodded, "Sole proprietor?"

"Yes, sir."

"And I gather you're asking for my advice?"

"Yes, sir."

"Well, although I think I know most of the details, I'll tell you what I tell my other clients. Start at the beginning and tell me everything." He chuckled. "I think we can work out some sort of reduced rate for the fee. Under the circumstances."

"The circumstances are that if it costs more than thirty-six dollars, I can't afford any legal advice."

Peter O'Hara frowned. "That bad, is it?"

"Yes, sir."

"Take it from the beginning, Dave," Pete said, and he sounded like a lawyer. He was sympathetic, but nothing could be done until all the facts were known.

Dave began. It had seemed like such a good idea when it started. Not only would they all have a fine time, but they would receive an excellent return on their money. Dave would be chief mechanic, and Charley Williams chief driver, and Joe Heller, Bryan Field, Dick Greenewald, and Al MacDondar, the pit team.

"Well, we started by each putting up five hunded dollars," Dave said. His five hundred dollars had been savings. He had started working at the gas station when he was a sophomore in high school, and had been vice-president in charge of windshield wiping and white sidewall cleaning. He didn't clean windshields any more—there were new sophomores for that job—and he pumped gas only when no one else was around. He spent his time in the shop. He had a real feeling for ignition and carburetion systems. It worked out very well. People dropped their cars off at the station after work, and Dave worked on them at night so that they were ready in the morning. He had started at 50 cents an hour. Now he worked on a 70-30 split, with Mr. Lewis, the owner, taking 30 percent for the use of the tools and the shop. It worked out well. Dave Wade's skill brought business to the station and the other functions of the garage, and Mr. Lewis' money had bought, among other things, the Stud-illac and the $500 share in Motor Enterprises.

He was so used to working for his own money that he had been surprised when he proposed Motor Enterprises that the others had had to borrow the $500 equal share from their parents. The only check deposited in their new bank account with the signature of a partner on it was Dave's. The others were all drawn on the bank accounts of the parents involved.

He had felt then that the parents were being 'nice,' not that they believed what he had to say. With a good stock car, and with Charley driving, they could make money. The parents gave him the impression that all of them were being patronized, that the group of them were 'nice boys,' and that $500 was a cheap enough price to keep them 'nice' and out of pool halls and roadhouses, away from 'evil companions.'

"And you formed a simple partnership?" Pete O'Hara asked.

"I suppose so," Dave said.

"A simple partnership is one in which all members are equal," Pete explained. "There is no senior partner, for example, and all expenses and profits are shared equally. Is that what you had?"

"Yes, sir."

"Did you have a termination covenant?"

"I don't even know what that means," Dave confessed.

"Supposing one of you had to, or just wanted to, get his money out?"

"Oh," Dave said. "Yes, sir. We had one of those. We agreed that after we'd won a couple of races and it looked as if we were going to make money, that, if anyone wanted to get out, the remaining members would give him his five hundred dollars back. We did that so no one would be tempted to make a profit."

"I see. Go ahead."

"Well, after the accident, they all wanted out," Dave said.

"That's a summation of what happened. I want all the

details."

It took Dave a moment to organize his thoughts. How do you tell a non-racer that what had happened was that a lead-footed idiot who shouldn't have been allowed on the track at all, driving a junker held together with glue, string, and hope, had spun out on the north turn of Race City Track, and that Charley Williams, already in a four-wheel slide, had slammed into him, clobbering the Motor Enterprises Special, demolishing the junker, and winding up in the hospital with a busted leg?

"Charley Williams," Dave said, "through no fault of his own, had a rather bad accident at the track. A car ahead of him was going too fast, and the driver lost control. Charley hit him."

Pete O'Hara nodded.

Dave, remembering the crash, thought it was completely understandable how Mrs. Williams felt. After they'd pried Charley out of the wreckage, and Dr. Nelson had found the broken leg, and they'd hauled him off to the hospital in an ambulance with the siren screaming, and they had started pulling the Motor Enterprises Special back to the pits, the junker had caught on fire. When its gasoline tank caught on fire, there had been a spectacular fire. That's what the *Evening News* had called it on the front page:

COLLEGE-STUDENT DRIVER HOSPITALIZED
AFTER SPECTACULAR FLAMING CRASH

"Charley Williams' leg is broken, isn't it?" Pete O'Hara asked.

"Yes, sir."

"What about his hospital bills? Who's going to pay those?"

"The track has some insurance," Dave said. "And we bought some more. He's covered. So is the guy he hit, as a matter of fact."

"Is he badly injured?"

"A couple of scratches," Dave said. "It was his fault and he didn't get hurt a tenth as much as Charley."

"With the exception of the leg, however, Charley will be all right?"

"Yes, sir. They said they'll have him on crutches in about a week."

"I hadn't realized, Dave, how dangerous this sport is," Pete O'Hara said. "I'm sure your mother will be glad you're out of it."

"Well, sir, I'm not out of it. And it's not really that dangerous," Dave said.

"That's neither here nor there, right now, Dave. Let's get back to Motor Enterprises."

"Well, Mr. and Mrs. Williams came to the hospital, of course. And so did some of the others. Mrs. Field and Mr. MacDondar were there before the Williamses when they heard about the accident on the radio."

"That was courteous of them."

"The announcer didn't say which one of us got hurt," Dave said.

"If your mother had heard that announcement, she would have been there, too," Pete said. "Frankly, I don't think you've got any cause to be annoyed with the other parents."

"Yes, sir," Dave said. "But . . ."

"But you didn't like being accused of being responsible for Charley getting hurt, is that it?"

"Yes, sir. How did you know about that?"

"Mr. MacDondar called here and said the same thing."

"Oh."

"I told him that I would speak sharply to you about forcing your will on poor, defenseless, none-too-bright Charley Williams," Pete O'Hara said, dryly. Charley Williams, in addition to being the best scholar of them all—had been on the Dean's List every quarter since entering college— was a full-back on the football team and loomed large even there. He outweighed Dave Wade by at least a hundred pounds. He did very little that he did not want to do, and everyone was aware of this.

"What happened was that when I walked in there with Bryan Field, his mother threw her arms around him and said that if he ever raced again, it would kill her, and that he was through. I don't think Bryan ever rode in that car, and I know he never drove it."

"And then she wanted her five hundred dollars back?"

"Yes, sir. It was like a chain reaction. First, Mrs. Field, and then Mr. MacDondar, and then Mr. Williams, and then Mr. Heller, and, finally, before we even got to see Charley, Mrs. Greenewald."

"And you had that much money?"

"No, sir. Not then. Still don't, really. There's some money coming in."

"Where's it coming from?"

"Well, we got starting money. That's two hundred and fifty, and Charley's lap money . . ."

"What's that?"

"That particular track pays five dollars for the man leading each lap. In other words, they make a little race within a race."

"Oh. How much is that?"

"About sixty or sixty-five dollars. He was doing well. And then, of course, the insurance money. That's probably about five hundred dollars."

"In other words, you have an anticipated income of between seven hundred and, say, nine hundred dollars."

"Yes, sir."

"You know, of course, Dave, that, under a partnership agreement such as the one you've detailed, you could have gone to them and asked for your five hundred dollars. It wasn't your legal obligation."

"Motor Enterprises was my idea," Dave said. "That made it my obligation."

"Not legally," Pete O'Hara insisted flatly. "It's what is known as a moral obligation. You may be broke, Dave, but you'll be able to look yourself in the mirror when you wash your face."

Dave didn't answer. They sat in silence for a full minute before O'Hara spoke again.

"What are you going to do, Dave?" he asked.

"Well," Dave said and then paused. "On the way down here, when I decided to talk it over with you, it seemed to be the only solution. But right now, I'm almost afraid to say it."

"Go ahead," Pete O'Hara said. "Nothing much shocks me any more about you and cars. Not since I made out your income tax for you, anyway."

"Well, I sort of put off telling Uncle Comer about going down there for the summer."

"I know. Your mother suggested to me that I suggest to you that you're right on the edge of very bad manners, not to mention hurting his feelings."

Uncle Comer was Comer Bragg Kerr, of Marianna, Florida, his mother's brother and proprietor of the Kerr Tractor, Farm Implement, Feed & Seed and Automobile Company of that city. Childless, his sister's kid-brother, he and Aunt Marge had issued an 'any time, for as long as you can stay' invitation to Dave to not only come to visit them, but to work at full wages in the garage.

"Yes, sir. I know."

"And now you've decided to go? I think that's a good idea. You might be able to recoup your losses. Comer's always awfully busy in the summer."

"Well, not just go," Dave said, hesitantly.

"Go and what, then?"

"Well, stock cars are big down in that part of the country. You've got Birmingham International Raceway, and the Atlanta Peachbowl, and Daytona and twenty-five or thirty smaller tracks. . . ." he stopped talking.

"Go on," Pete O'Hara said. "You've already started. That's half the battle."

"Well, really race," Dave said.

"Who would you get to drive the Special. I gather you're talking about fixing the Special?"

"There's not much wrong with the Special. Couple of hundred dollars worth of parts, and it'll run."

"If you sold it, how much would you get?"

"Once a car is wrecked, the price drops sharply until it's repaired and then raced a couple of times. Raced and placed or won. I don't think I could sell the whole works, car, trailer, spare engines, all of it, for two thousand dollars right now."

"And if you get it back in shape, and race it, and it's won a couple of times, then how much?"

"Four, five thousand. Plus what the purses would be. They have good purses. Three, four, even five hundred dollars a race."

"Who would drive it? You'd have to pay him."

"I would," Dave said, raising his head to look his stepfather and friend in the eye.

"Oh," Pete O'Hara said. Now he moved. He took the thick law book from his lap, and put it on the table. Then he took his glasses off and folded them, and put them in his breast pocket. Then he turned and looked at Dave.

"You don't scare easy, do you?" he asked. "Doesn't Charley in the hospital make you think?"

"It makes me think, but not the way you'd guess," Dave said, and then it came out in a rush. "It makes me think that I wouldn't have wrecked it that way. It makes me think I've always been the better driver." Now he was embarrassed. "I guess that makes me sound like I'm the original guy with the big head, doesn't it?"

"No," Pete O'Hara said. "As a matter of fact, from the spectators' seats, I formed the same opinion."

"I didn't know you went to the races," Dave said.

"Fair's fair," Pete O'Hara said. "You didn't tell me you were racing, I didn't feel it necessary to tell you I was watching. I guess I really hoped you would give it up."

"Now I'm ashamed of myself," Dave said.

"You should be, I think, a little bit," O'Hara said. "That was almost cheating, Dave, You didn't try to hide it, but neither did you spread it around very much."

"I didn't want to worry Mom," Dave said.

"How do you think she's going to react to this?" O'Hara asked.

"Well, that settles that," Dave said. "I just won't do it."

Pete O'Hara pursed his lips. Then he said, "That'll be up to your mother."

"Well, she'd certainly ask you," Dave replied.

"If she asks me, Dave," Pete O'Hara said, "I will tell her that, as a strictly business proposition, your idea has merit. I will tell her that it will give you valuable experience that you could get in no other way for your choice of a career. I happen to believe that business that most automobile safety features, starting with four-wheel brakes, were born on the auto race track. I will tell her that Comer will watch you with even more of an expert eye than I can."

"Gee . . ." Dave said, and Pete O'Hara stopped him by raising his hand. "I'm not through. I will remind her that your father had a 1939 Ford with a 1941 Cadillac engine that was the fastest car on the highways, and that she went on her honeymoon in a high performance automobile. But most important, Dave, I'll tell her that I think you've proved you're a man, and that a man has to be allowed to do what he thinks he should do."

"Gee, Pete, thanks."

"I'm not saying that she'll agree with this, Dave. And maybe, deep inside, I hope she doesn't. I don't want them scraping you off a race track, either. But, I understand, and I think you're right. I'll take her out to dinner tonight and break it to her gently. That is, if I can enlist you as the cook and babysitter for the rest of the family?"

"Yes, sir," Dave said.

Two

AROUND TOWN, and as far away as Langhorne and Chester and Valley Stream, the Motor Enterprises Special had been hauled around on its trailer behind Mr. Lewis' pickup truck. That had been sort of a fringe benefit of Dave Wade's employment at the gas station and a little advertising for the station itself. I didn't hurt Mr. Lewis' business at all to have people associate the Motor Enterprises Special with Lewis' Super Service.

But the Lewis Super Service Chevrolet pickup certainly could not be used to haul the motor Enterprise Special to Marianna, Florida, now that somewhat reluctant permission for Dave to go had been granted.

Logically, it was easy to decide, and the path was clear before him. Since he had to tow a wrecked, stock-car racer 1,000 miles, carrying with him as many of its spare parts, and all his hand tools, and two spare engines, what he needed was a truck. Since he did not have a truck, he would have to buy a truck. Since he did not have enough money to buy a truck, he would have to sell something to get the money. Since he did not need the Stud-illac (and certainly couldn't drive both the Stud-illac and a truck at the same time) it was obvious that the choice had been made for him. The Stud-illac would have to go.

Personally, it wasn't quite that simple. There was no way to tell how many hundreds of hours of loving labor had gone into the Stud-illac. Or how many memories were associated with it since he had acquired title from the P. Dennacropolis & Son Used Auto Parts and Junkyard three years before. It had been then what insurance company slang calls a 'totalled.' It had been in a wreck.

In the solemn and professional opinion of the insurance investigator and his superior, the insurance adjuster, the car had been so badly damaged that repair, while not impossible, was impractical. For one thing, the power train was bent beyond correction. For another, the telephone pole which had brought the car to an abrupt stop had changed the shape of the radiator from flat to U- shaped, and jammed the fan tight against the engine, pulling the engine block off the engine mounts.

It was, in other words, a total loss to the insurance company. The original owner had been paid in full and had gone off to a new car. And after Mr. Dennacropolis had peeled off a twenty dollar bill from a thick, greasy roll of them carried in the pocket of his thick, greasy coveralls and handed it reluctantly to the insurance adjuster, title to it had been transferred to him, and a rubber stamp marked

CLAIM CLOSED—TOTALLED had, in everybody's opinion but that of seventeen-year-old David Wade, marked the official end of that particular product of the Studebaker Corporation.

Maybe the radio could be sold. Or the wheels. Or someone would need a windshield, or just a windshield wiper. Mr. Dennacropolis might or might not get his twenty dollars back before the totalled wreck wound up between the jaws of the crusher and started back toward the steel mill. That was the way it was in the junk business.

David Wade entered the life of the Studebaker at the time when everyone felt the life of that particular Studebaker was absolutely, if sadly, over. Specifically, he had seen it on the way to school, and he had almost been late to school, because he had stopped horrified to see wrapped around a telephone pole what he felt quite sure was the automobile with the finest lines since the 1941 Lincoln Continental.

He was so fascinated that he got down on his knees and looked under the car to see how much damage had been done. At first, his worst suspicions seemed to be realized. The engine had been shoved back to the fire wall, and that (coupled with the visible bend in the drive shaft and the ruptured transmission housing) certainly spelled a bent frame.

But he looked closer. The engine support bolts had sheared, not the supports themselves. That could happen, he guessed, if the car had hit as squarely as this one had hit. With that in mind, he looked inside the car. It was in good shape inside. With the exception of the crumpled hood and right fender, the body was in good shape. The steering wheel was badly bent, but not the steering-wheel pedestal.

He thought about the car most of that day in school, which, while it did not endear him to his teachers, was passed over by them as an infrequent lapse into girl-considering by an otherwise calm-headed A student. It would be overlooked.

After school, changed into the blue-and-white Lewis Super Service uniform, he found himself still thinking about what he now considered to be a slightly damaged jewel.

"Mr. Lewis, could you let me have fifty dollars?"

"Sure," Mr. Lewis said, reaching for his checkbook, eyeing Dave as the teachers had eyed him, knowing that something was out of the ordinary, but, because Dave was an honest, hard-working, bright youngster, deciding it was best to stay out of it for the time being.

"No, sir," Dave Wade said, nodding at the check book. "I mean cash a check for me, please. And I'd like to take the truck for about half-an-hour, if I could."

"What are you going to buy?"

"I saw a car I'd like to have."

"For fifty dollars?"

"Well, yes, sir. It's worth that. But I think if I had more than that with me, I'd pay more. That's why I want fifty dollars in cash."

Mr. Lewis shrugged, and handed him the money as Dave wrote out the check.

"I'll be back right away. No more than half-an-hour." he said.

"Take your time. Things are always slow on Monday anyhow."

His first stop was the police station. He stood fairly high in the somewhat harsh judgment of the police for high school seniors. After the police mechanic had failed completely to do so, Dave had been able, by using newly developed spark suppressers, to remove almost all of an annoying (maddening, according to Sergeant Hess) hiss on the police radios. To policemen who spent six to ten hours a day listening to the radio, he was sort of an adoloscent leprechaun.

"Hello, Dave," Sergeant Hess called from a doorway as a new and unknown policeman behind the desk gave Dave the curious and somehow cold and unfriendly glance given teen-agers in police stations.

"Hello, Sergeant Hess."

"Is this a social call, or do we owe you money again?"

"No, sir. I wanted a little information. Where'd they haul that wrecked Studebaker?"

"That '59 coupe that guy clobbered the pole with?"

"Yes, sir."

"Over to the Greek's. Why?"

"I'm going to try to buy it," Dave said.

"It's totaled," Sergeant Hess said. "Are we talking about the same car?"

"Unless there's more than one '59 coupe."

"What are you going to do with it? Put it on the roof of the gas station as an attention-getter?"

"No, sir. I think I can fix it."

Sergeant Hess had no further comment to make aloud. His raised, bushy eyebrow made it for him. But when Dave left, he walked to the desk and reached up and took the telephone from the cradle."

"Dial the Greek for me, will you?" he said to the officer on duty.

He learned from Mr. Dennacropolis that it was Mr. Dennacropolis' opinion that he was no smarter now than when they had been in the fifth grade together. For one thing, P. Dennacropolis was not so hungry for money that he had to go around cheating high school kids, especially high school kids like Dave Wade, who was a nice kid. And for another, it was P. Dennacropolis' opinion that Dave Wade, of all people, didn't need any thick-headed cop to tell him anything about cars.

"If you tell Charley Lewis I said this, Al," Mr. Dennacropolis said, "I'll deny it. But I would just as soon have that seventeen-year-old kid work on my engine as anybody I know, including Charley Lewis. He's got a feel for it. You know what I mean? If I didn't figure it would get his pride all in an uproar, I'd give him this wreck."

Title to the 1959 Studebaker coupe passed from P. Dennacropolis & Son Used Auto Parts and Junkyard to David Wade, for, and in consideration of Twenty Dollars and No Cents, in cash.

It took him four months to get it to the point where he thought he could get it past the eagle-eyed inspectors at the State Inspection Station. These worthy gentlemen, not aware that Dave Wade believed in important things first, were rather surprised to find that the rolling wreck which squeaked and clattered into the inspection bay was sort of automotive proof that externals are unimportant.

Beneath the rusty, bent, and torn hood, and beside the ripped, rusty and hammer-battered left fender, was a Cadillac engine which purred and ticked like a contented cat who had swallowed a Swiss watch. There was no covering on the floor boards, and the angry marks of acetylene torch burning and electric welding marked the outside of a revamped, enlarged transmission tunnel. But beneath the metallic stitching and patching rested, securely, a four-speed, Borg-Warner transmission.

There were new and heavy duty shock absorbers fore and aft, and when the car was run onto brake tester, the brakes tested eight points better than the car just before it, which would that afternoon be delivered from a new car showroom.

"Can I ask you a question, Fella?" the Inspection Service corporal asked.

"Yes, sir."

"With all of that underneath, why does it look so. . . ."

"Lousy?"

"You said it, not me."

"I ran out of money," Dave said. "I had to borrow two hundred dollars from my stepfather for the transmission. I'll get the hood and fender replaced."

"Well, you pass. It's safe. Frankly, it's the safest thing I've checked lately. But I don't think it will win any beauty prizes."

"Wait till I come back," Dave said.

[27]

The Stud-illac was more than a car. It had become a part of his life. And there was a great deal of money in it, not only in terms of his labor, but in parts, even at the wholesale cost.

There was a great deal more money in it than he would be able to get out of it. And yet he couldn't feel sorry for himself as the facts of automobile life were explained to him. He knew enough about the facts himself, moreover, and knew that the reason Mr. Henschel of Henschel Motors was successful was because he had earned a reputation for being honest over more years than Dave's age.

"Dave, no matter how you slice it, it's a five-year-old car. Now you know, and in this particular case, I know, that not only is this a fast car, but a safe and reliable car. But put yourself in the position of one of my salesmen. Would you believe him if he told you that the reason this car is on the used-car lot is because the owner needed a truck, and not because it was a worn-out hot rod?"

"No, sir, I guess not."

"I'll give you *Blue Book*, Dave, on anything you want I've got. That's the best I can do."

• *Blue Book* was the monthly report of used car prices published, more or less confidentially, by the Automobile Dealer's Association.

On the way from the passenger car showroom to the truck showroom, they passed through what once had been the entire garage for Henschel Motor Company, and what now was sort of an automobile warehouse. The last time Dave had passed through here, it had been full of brand-new, if somewhat dusty, automobiles, fresh from the assembly plant.

Today it was full of orange, yellow, and red trucks. On each side of the hood Dave could see a full color drawing of a steaming pizza. He could not see the truck sides, the way the trucks were parked, but he had seen the trucks enough to know what was there: a drawing of a smiling chef with a pizza in his hands, and the words, LUIGI'S NEAPOLITAN PIZZA!! Like Mama Made!!"

The trucks, and there were more than a dozen of them, were used to haul frozen pizzas from the factory to restaurants and diners all over town, or from time to time (at the state and county fairs, or at the baseball and football games) to sell hot pizzas directly from the truck to individual consumers.

He thought that Luigi, whoever he and his mama were, must be making some money. Those trucks didn't look worn out at all, and here they were trading them for new. And then he thought about that again. They didn't look worn out at all.

"Have those been traded, Mr. Henschel?"

"Uh huh."

"What kind of shape are they in?"

"Oh!" Mr. Henschel said, as he understood Dave's path of thought. "Want to take a look?"

"Yes, sir. If I can."

The first thing Dave looked for was the interior size. When he'd checked this, he checked the suspension system. He would be taking two spare engines with him. Spare engines are heavy.

Thirty-five minutes later, Dave Wade left Henschel motors driving a truck. When he got home, there was some bitter disappointment on the part of his half-brother and his half-sister that a pizza was not forthcoming. He had to go get them some.

He thought he was probably the only man in the world who had ever driven a pizza truck out to buy a pizza. And he thought he was a pretty childish type, when you got right down to it, for he had been actually very close to tears when he'd emptied the glove compartment of the Stud-illac and turned over the keys to Mr. Henschel.

His mother showed signs, that last night, of getting sentimental, but Peter O'Hara had joked her out of it. And she agreed, after some prodding, that it did make sense for him to leave very early in the morning so that he could get onto the interstate highway before the morning traffic began.

So the good-nights were really good-byes. He went to bed early so as to get a good night's sleep, and later decided that, added all together, he probably got as much as an hour's sleep, two or three minutes at a time.

He didn't make good time, for a number of reasons. First, the Luigi's Neapolitan pizza truck had a gear train designed to haul pizzas around a city at the best possible gasoline mileage, rather than travel at highway speeds. Conversely, this low gear-ratio permitted the trailer to be towed putting little strain on the truck. But you can't tow anything rapidly and safely.

Since the Motor Enterprises Special represented all of

Dave Wade's capital assets, and he was fully aware of this, he drove with great caution.

He stopped for breakfast when he was thirty miles out of town, and was surprised at the size of his appetite. For the last couple of days, he hadn't had any appetite at all to speak of. But now, with the menu before him and the smells coming from the kitchen, he knew that he simply could not do with less than the Number Two Special breakfast, which was orange juice, two hotcakes, sausage, two eggs, toast, jelly, and coffee. And even as he ordered this, he recognized that it had not been designed with his stomach in mind.

"To go with that, please," he said to the waitress, "I'll have a large glass of milk, and you'd better scramble about four eggs instead of two. And maybe you'd better give me an order of french fried potatoes."

He ate all of it and, halfway through his meal, had the large glass of milk refilled.

I really do . . . he thought, as he stood up, paid his bill and walked outside, I really feel like a new man.

He understood what it was. Now that he was actually on the way to Uncle Comer, now that the first step had been taken, there was nothing really to worry about, for he knew it made no sense to worry about those things he couldn't control. Since there was nothing to worry about, there was no nervous tension to affect his appetite. The appetite was back, and making up for lost time.

By eleven fifteen, he was hungry again. He pulled off the highway and had two super-giant double-burgers and another order of french fried potatoes, washing it all down with a colossal-sized, chocolate malted milk.

After lunch, he drank a leisurely cup of coffee and then crawled into a pair of coveralls. He crawled first under the truck, checking the trailer-hitch for signs of looseness and metal fatigue, then the truck's springs and shock absorbers to see how they had borne up under the weight of the two spare engines and the disorganized collection of spare parts.

When he was satisfied with the condition of the truck, he untied the nylon drop cloth over the Motor Enterprises Special. In the daylight, it looked even worse than it had the day of the accident, or since, when he'd looked at it in garages. The wreck had happened just long enough ago so that the bare metal of the body, exposed during the accident, was now rust covered. Fuel and oil had spilled on other parts of the wrecked car, and since the accident, had acted like magnets, picking up dust from the air and turning it into greasy dirt.

Looking at it, he had to remind himself that the car wasn't as hopeless as it looked, that it had been, from the view of a mechanic, a spectacular, rather than a ruinous accident. It could be fixed. It would be fixed.

Even as he began to check the trailer springs, the air pressure in the trailer tires, and the electrical connections, he was already considering how he would go about rebuilding it and wondering if Uncle Comer really had a well equipped shop.

Then he tied the drop cloth over the wrecked car again, checked the lights-and-brake connector one final time, and got behind the wheel of the truck.

When there was room in the line of traffic, he pulled back onto the highway, managing to ignore the look of puzzled fascination on the face of a young man in a car, a young man who apparently had never been previously privileged to see a wrecked stock car being hauled along a superhighway by a truck marked, Luigi's Neapolitan Pizza.

_____ Three

ALTHOUGH HE HAD never been personally responsible for a major accident, David Wade's experience with highway catastrophe was somewhat broader than that of the average young man on the brink of his official majority. He had long ago lost count of the number of accidents to which he had driven Mr. Lewis' wrecker, and had even lost count of the number of accidents he'd gone to preceded by the flashing, red light and howling scream of a police siren, because a wrecker was needed to pull crash-bent doors open before the injured could be removed.

He had developed, without really being aware that he was considering the matter at all, what really was "David Wade's Theory of the Cause of Highway Accidents."

Any fool could understand that drunken driving was a major cause, and it required no thought whatever to arrive at a solution. Put people who drive while drunk in jail. But he understood that by no means were all, or even a substantial majority of highway accidents, caused by so simple a cause as a drunk.

He had seen fatal and near fatal accidents involving responsible people who had never had a drink in their lives, and who were driving new and nearly new cars. He did not believe (and, talking it over with some of his friends on the police force and the highway patrol, found that, privately, neither did they) that the second major cause of accidents was speeding.

It was far more complex than just that. You could say, of course, that accidents were caused by people driving too fast for conditions. Conditions was a large word, taking in any number of things. And how fast is 'too fast'?

He didn't like to say it out loud even with people who would probably respect his opinion, and would not decide that he was simply a young man with a large and loud mouth. But after drunken driving as a cause of accidents, he listed driving by people who really should not be entrusted with automobiles that powerful, who did not understand the power they commanded.

All the cartoons showed the ladies as those who knew nothing about the mechanics of automobiles, who would put gasoline in the radiator and marvel at the rear-engined Volkswagen because it didn't have an engine up front.

But Dave knew many men whose ignorance of things automotive matched that of any woman. He knew men who publicly announced that stock-car racing was dangerous and should be outlawed, but who thought nothing whatever of driving 200 miles at 70 miles an hour on worn-smooth tires, or the same 200 miles at the same speed with worn-out brakes, because it had been inconvenient for them to have the brakes relined, and it could be done when they got back.

He knew men who would boast that on a deserted road on a moonlight night (so it would be safe), they had 'opened her up, to see what she would do,' proud of the power of their engines and blissfully unaware that the moment they passed 70 miles an hour on unsafe, bargain tires they were quite frankly flirting with blowouts, major accidents, and death itself.

He was sure that when he had gotten behind the wheel of the Motor Enterprises Special, with new, expensive, racing tires on the wheels, thick, new brake lining, new shock absorbers, a roll-bar, a seat belt and shoulder harness, that he was really a great deal safer than many people who loaded wife, children and Grandma into the family car for a ride in the country on Sunday.

No one, however, except other people who really knew (other race drivers, mechanics, and some of the police) would believe this. They didn't want to believe it, because it was an unpleasant truth.

Of all the people who drove non-professionally, so to speak, he had found that truck drivers and traveling salesmen, probably because they drove so much, were generally safe drivers, not only skillful, but cautious in terms of brakes and tires and speed.

Because the answer to this was so simple, it took him a long time to figure out why truck drivers and traveling salesmen had accidents. It wasn't just a matter of percentage. And it wasn't simply that they had failed to avoid being run down by unskilled drivers.

The reason they had accidents despite a high skill level and good cars and trucks was that they drove long distances and got tired, and the reflexes of tired people slow down.

These were not just the idle opinions of Dave Wade, something he thought about when there was nothing much else to consider. He lived by them. He would not ride in a car with bad brakes, or in one with smooth tires, or a loose front end. He had seen too many dead and seriously injured people to be embarrassed to refuse.

And so, just north of Atlanta at five o'clock in the afternoon, with at least another three hours of daylight to go, and, according to the road map, on good roads, Dave Wade started looking for a nice motel. He was tired, and he simply did not drive when he was tired. He had been driving twelve hours.

"Where's your car?" the motel proprietor asked, curiously.

"I . . . uh . . ." Dave said, and then gestured through the plate-glass window toward the truck and the trailer.

"Oh," the proprietor said and examined him carefully. Dave felt that the man would have been happier if he had gone elsewhere, but couldn't think of what to say to him to make him leave. "That'll be eight dollars," he said, and when Dave gave him a ten dollar bill, he examined it carefully before making change.

The room was so pleasant and so clean that it was easy to

forget the nagging suspicion that he wasn't welcome. There was a shower with plenty of hot water, and then an adequate supply of thick, soft towels. He shaved himself, put on a clean white shirt, a pair of clean (if somewhat worn and faded) khakis, a light sport coat, and decided that what he needed was a good, filling meal. And then the television for a couple of hours, something to read when television became just too much to take, a good night's rest on what obviously would be a comfortable mattress, and then, off again very early in the morning. He could make Uncle Comer's by the following night.

Before he left the room he called home as he promised he would do. It wasn't as difficult as he thought it would be. He got the impression that (once having learned he was alive and in good health) his mother was really glad to have him out of the house. He decided, when all things were considered, that he must be something of a nuisance.

There was a delightful sense of freedom now, after he had spoken with the kids and, finally, Peter O'Hara and hung up. He was foot-loose and fancy free. He was alone, and there was something delightful in being alone. While he was sure that the feeling would pass, and that he would get terribly hungry for the house and even for the kids, at the moment, he was frankly glad to be separated from all of them.

The motel boasted a restaurant, and the chef was obviously the proprietor's wife, for when he ordered dinner her face appeared at the diamond-shaped window in the kitchen door. While he was waiting for the food to be served, he went to a rack and bought the newspaper, the *Atlanta Times*. For reasons he somehow mistrusted, his mother was against people reading at the table. It was only on a rare Saturday morning when she was still in bed that he and Pete were permitted to spread the paper beside them and feed both the mind and the body simultaneously.

It was entirely pleasant and satisfying to be able to lay the paper out in the sure knowledge that it was his unquestioned right to do so.

The portions served weren't very large, and, as he read the paper, he thought that he would probably have to order a second whole dinner, because this obviously wasn't going to be enough for a man who had driven all day.

He was methodical. He read the paper from front to back, reading everything, from international news to financial reports, and even studying with an interested eye the Women's Section, which consisted almost entirely of slightly out-of-focus photographs of local belles who were announcing their engagements.

They all look, he thought, either like sleepy angels or determined saints about to embark on a noble crusade of some sort. He thought that newspaper photographs of brides-to-be were proof positive that pictures lied.

The brides' pictures were next to last in the paper. Last were the classified ads, and he even scanned these. And then he looked up. The proprietor's wife was standing there looking down at him and smiling.

"Yes, ma'am?"

"Are you still hungry?"

He almost answered without thinking, but stopped. Funny thing was, he was sure he was going to be hungry, but now he seemed to have enough. As a matter of fact, he thought, I'm stuffed.

"No, ma'am," he said. "Thank you. I seem to be full. It was very good."

"Didn't you have any lunch?" she asked.

"Yes, ma'am. I had lunch. Why do you ask?"

"You had three helpings of meat and potatoes, and that was the fifth dish of lima beans. You also ate six slices of bread."

He felt himself flushing, and then she laughed.

"Don't be embarrased," she said. "I consider it a compliment, if you really did eat lunch."

"Yes, ma'am."

"You have deep powers of concentration," she said. "That's valuable."

"The truth of the matter is," he said, now speaking without thinking. "My mother doesn't let me read at the table."

"I can see why," she said, and laughed, and then, "What is that you're towing behind your pizza wagon?"

"That's a stock car," he said.

"You're a stock-car racer?" she asked.

"Yes, ma'am," he said. It was true. But saying it aloud for the first time gave him pleasure.

"In town for the races?" she said.

"No, ma'am. The car on the trailer is a wreck. I'm headed for Marianna, Florida. My uncle has a garage there, and I'm going to rebuild it."

"Well," she said. "I hated to interrupt your newspaper reading, but I thought maybe I'd better before you ate up this year's profits."

He felt himself flushing.

"I'm just needling you," she said. "You don't see an appetite like that much, even in a restaurant any more."

"I didn't mean to make a pig of myself," he said.

"The track isn't far," she said, changing the subject. "And they start time trials in about half-an-hour."

"Thank you," he said. He would go. Watching racing, even from the stands, pushed the idea of watching television and then going to bed early from his mind.

She gave him a marked road map when he paid his dinner check. He was somewhat embarrassed after her recitation of how many helpings he had had that his bill was so small.

"I haven't seen anyone eat like that since my husband when we were first married," she said and Dave understood that somehow his bottomless stomach really gave her pleasure.

He unhitched the trailer from the truck and set off down the highway. It was easy to find the track, even without the map she'd given him or the signs along the road. There was a steady stream of cars filled with young people headed toward it. They were generally very well-polished, and many of them had NASCAR or USAC stickers in the windows.

He had seen crowds like this one before. He knew he was headed in the right direction.

He stopped in line outside the track parking lot, resigned

to a good ten minutes of moving eight feet and stopping, and then moving eight feet again. But this wasn't to happen. He became aware first of the angry blast of a police whistle, and was still wondering why the wrong-doer hadn't either stopped what was apparently offending the law or the law hadn't arrested him, when he was shocked with the sudden realization that the whistle was being blown at him.

This was brought to his attention by an officer of the law who jerked open the already half-open sliding door to the truck, and inquired,

"What's the matter with you, Mac? Are you deaf or something?"

And then he pulled his head out of the truck as quickly as he had put it in, backed away from the truck, resumed his furious blasts on the whistle, and gestured violently for Dave to pull out of his lane into the adjacent lane, and to do so with the greatest possible haste.

Dave wondered what he had done that was apparently going to have him taken to the police station.

The lane into which he now moved led beyond the parking lots and to a tunnel beneath the track itself. On a billboard close to the track, Dave had seen the prices posted, and the inside of the track, the paddock, was more expensive than the bleachers outside.

Ahead was a ticket booth. Well, he would simply tell the ticket taker that he did not want to go in the paddock, that he wanted to go in the parking lot where he had been headed when the law spoke up.

But he was not given this opportunity, either. The ticket

taker at the ticket booth just waved him on, smiled cheerfully, and said, "How are you, today?"

Utterly confused, Dave let out the clutch and drove through the tunnel. When he came out, he saw that the paddock was lined with parked cars, but that no one who looked as though he was collecting admissions was in sight. Halfway down the mass of parked cars, he realized what had happened. The cop and the ticket taker had seen Luigi's Neapolitan Pizza on the sides of the truck, and, rather understandably, decided that Dave was on hand professionally as a vendor of Neopolitan pizza rather than as a ticket-buying member of the public.

He laughed. At least he could say his conscience was clear. He had not sneaked into the track. He had been ordered in by a policeman and greeted warmly by a member of the staff. He decided that he would only compound the confusion by trying to explain it to someone.

He pulled the truck into a vacant space—saw there weren't many left—and got out. The moment he was outside the truck, he smelled the odor of racing, of new rubber and burned rubber, of fresh oil and of oil that had vaporized on a hot exhaust manifold, of fresh automotive lacquer, and of racing suits dipped in borax and boric acid to make them flame proof.

Still somewhat off balance after the policeman's whistle-blasting, he walked toward the pits without much considering that he, first, had no business there, and, second, was fully aware that extra people in the pits are not only in the way but can often be actually troublesome. He had gone past a couple of junkers and was listening with an attentive ear to a Pontiac 425 with ignition problems when he was again rudely made aware that someone wanted his attention.

"What's your name, Buddy? Bill France?"

Dave was fully aware that Mr. William France was president of the National Association for Stock Car Racing, and he was fully aware that Mr. France was a gentleman in his fifties. Finally, he was aware that everybody even remotely connected with racing was familiar with Mr. France's smiling, fifty-year-old face. This excited, little, fat guy with an official's brassard was being sarcastic.

"My name is Wade," he said.

"And I suppose you got a license, but left it home, huh?" the little official said.

"Not only do I have a license, but I have it with me," Dave said, and took out his wallet and laid several cards one on top of the other in his hand. First was the NASCAR driver's licenses, and the next the NASCAR owner's certificate, and after that the NASCAR registered official's credentials certifying that Dave was qualified to serve as technical inspector, director of communications, and timer. And finally, his FIA and USAC licenses, which identified him as a driver qualified to race in races carried out under the supervision of the *Federation Internationale d'Automobile*, and as a member of the United States Automobile Club.

"So I'm sorry," the little official said.

"Forget it."

"We get so many helpful volunteers in the pits it's a miracle we don't run one over every hour."

"I'm about to get out myself," Dave said, somewhat embarrassed.

"We'd appreciate it," the official said. "We don't ask guys with licenses to go, but, frankly, unless they got something to do, we'd just as soon not have them in the pits."

"I'll go," Dave said.

"Could you tell me something?" the official asked. He was friendly now, having accepted Dave as a member of the fraternity.

"Sure?"

"What is that pizza truck, a gag of some kind?"

"I'm going to enter it against Dick Petty at the Daytona 500," Wade said.

The official laughed, and then Dave told him the story of Luigi's Neapolitan pizza truck, and this, of course, identified him as a visitor, passing through.

"Walk around with me if you like," the official said, putting out his hand, identifying himself, "I'll show you what we've got. I've got to prowl the pits anyway."

"Thanks," Dave said. "I'd like that."

He knew that in the company of an official, he would be unlikely to be challenged by another official.

By the time they had walked the length of the pits, the excited, fat, little guy had become a nice fellow who happened to be a little plump. His name was Roger Chedister, Dave learned, and he was to be a senior at Georgia Tech. He was going into the automobile industry when he graduated, like Dave, and, like Dave, he couldn't at the moment say what branch of the industry.

But it was obvious that they were kindred souls. By their second trip through the pits (during which Roger evicted six people) Dave had told Roger of his plans for the wrecked Motor Enterprises Special, and they had exchanged addresses.

Dave had the odd feeling that he and Roger had known one another for a long time.

When the time trials were over and the racing was about to be begin, Roger Chedister had to leave. They shook hands, for they seemed to understand without having to say it that they would see one another again, but not that day. Roger was working, and Dave was a spectator and nonparticipant.

His free admission troubled his conscience somewhat, and he decided that while it would be fruitless to try to explain what had happened to a busy track official, he could make up for it somehow by admitting to himself that, despite the smells and the proximity to the cars, the best place to watch a race from was a grandstand.

He walked through a pedestrian tunnel and to a ticket window, and laid down $3.30 for a reserved seat in the grandstand. It was, he reflected, the most money he had ever paid to watch a race.

It was a good seat, too, fifty yards or so to the right of the start-finish line and just high enough so that he could see just about all of the track, and not so high that it appeared to be something seen from the window of an airliner. From a vendor he bought a hot dog and a large root beer, settled himself comfortably against the backrest and prepared to watch the race.

If the 490 HP on the hood of that Pontiac meant 490 Horsepower, it should be a real bomb, even faster than that low-slung Olds.

"Will you excuse me, please?" a female voice said, and he turned in impatience to remain in fascination. And then, aware that he had been staring for a least ten full seconds, he scrambled to his feet.

"Certainly," he said. "Pardon me." She was a blonde, and he thought that blondes were just dandy, especially when they gave every appearance of having come by their golden locks naturally and without the ministrations of the beautician. This one, obviously, was a natural blonde. He could see her hair down to the roots, and it was blonde all the way. Her eyebrows were blonde, and her eyes were deep and blue.

The eyes of the young man with her were gray, interested, and unfriendly.

"The race is down there," the young man with her said. "On that streetlike thing down there."

"Sorry," Dave Wade said, and got to his feet and moved four seats away. With a great deal of effort, he kept from looking at the blonde for about five minutes.

"I think you're in my seat, Buddy," a middle aged man said apologetically, and Dave remembered that these were reserved seats. He moved back where he had been before.

The young man with the blonde looked at him again, his

stare just as unfriendly as before.

"I've got to sit here," Dave said, awkwardly. "Reserved seats, you see."

"I always had the impression that you could avoid the riffraff in reserved seats," the young man said.

I should take a poke at you for that, Dave thought. Except that by staring at the blonde, I wasn't exactly a well-behaved young gentleman. Furthermore, if I did belt you one, that would embarrass the blonde, and I wouldn't want to do that. I wouldn't embarrass her, even for the great satisfaction of taking a poke at you.

He said nothing.

The girl said, "Oh, be quiet, Rufus."

As the races were run Dave overheard Rufus talking. Rufus, apparently, did a little racing himself. To hear Rufus tell it, he was pretty good, much better than the racers out there on the track doing their pathetic best.

Dave also got the idea that the blonde believed what he felt was unadulterated hot air, and this would have really upset him if it weren't for his strange belief that the blonde had, not once, not even twice, but three times smiled shyly at him.

The next time he glanced in her direction, Rufus was gone. He had been so determined not to be caught staring at her again as though she was a bicycle and he was a seven-year-old boy that he hadn't even seen Rufus go.

And now he was sure she was smiling at him.

"Rufus is a race driver," she said.

"So am I," Dave blurted.

"Oh?" her eyebrows went up and he sensed that she didn't believe him.

"I'm an owner-driver," he said. "With NASCAR, USAC and FIA licenses."

"I see," she said, and now he knew she didn't believe him. He was reaching for his wallet to show her when out of the corner of his eye he saw Rufus coming down the stairway again.

He was whipped, and he knew he was whipped. He got up and walked to the stairs. He and Rufus glowered at each other as they passed, Dave headed down and Rufus on his way up.

Dave watched the rest of the races from inside the paddock and then waited about thirty minutes, hoping to see Roger Chedister again. There were several hundred things a race official could be doing at the end of a race, and so he found the truck and started out of the paddock.

Three lines of cars converged at the point where the track entrance met the highway. A policeman efficiently and impartially fed one car at a time into the one departing lane. It was efficient but slow. When Dave finally reached the head of his line, he glanced idly out the door. Two lines away, in a new, fire-engine red Thunderbird convertible sat Rufus and the blonde. And the blonde was looking at him and at the still livid Luigi's Neapolitan Pizza painted on the truck.

Dave Wade succeeded with some effort in refraining from banging his head against the steering wheel in rage and frustration. He knew what the blonde must think of a guy who said he was a NASCAR, USAC and FIA racer, but who drove a pizza truck.

He was grateful when Rufus' turn came first, and the Thunderbird went down the highway. If he had been first, the Thunderbird would have passed him a second time.

Four

THE PROPRIETOR'S WIFE
was on duty in the kitchen again
when Dave went to the motel restaurant early the next morning. When he ordered eggs sunny side up with a side order of bacon, she served him four eggs and what must have been a pound of bacon. This served to dull the embarrassment he still felt from the confrontation of the pizza wagon and red Thunderbird of the night before.

And when he paid his bill, and she said, "Stop by again whenever you're near Atlanta," he felt that she meant it, that she really would like to see him again, that it was something more than a ritual statement to a customer by someone in business.

When he considered that his appetite and her generosity with her food had certainly wiped out whatever margin of profit she had from the motel rental, he was sure that she meant it, and this made him feel good, for he had already learned that making friends was always pleasant but not something one could do everyday.

The four-way highway which had brought him to Atlanta petered out 20 miles south of that city, the smooth wide concrete giving way to a two-lane, well-traveled, macadam road. It took him about three hours to cover the 100 miles to Columbus, including the thirty minutes he spent in Columbus eating an even dozen ten-cent hamburgers in the Crystal Tower Hamburger stand.

He crossed into Alabama at Columbus, moving from Columbus, Georgia, into Phenix City, Alabama. Pete O'Hara had been stationed at Fort Benning, outside Columbus, and had still remembered enough about Phenix City to warn Dave about it twenty-three years later.

"Keep your eyes on the road, your hand on your wallet, and your mouth shut," Pete had said.

The warning seemed foolish. Phenix City looked calm, clean and very respectable. After the Attorney General of Alabama had been murdered, outraged citizens had thrown the gamblers and the bootleggers in jail, and several years later elected John Patterson, son of the Attorney General, to be Governor.

Dave thought that he would have that much to tell Pete in a letter or on the telephone. He certainly didn't want to get into reporting what he had said to the nameless blonde and what a fool he had obviously appeared to be.

By the time he was out of Phenix City, on Alabama U.S. 431, he had put the blonde firmly, finally, and once and for all from his mind.

It was almost exactly 100 miles from Phenix City to

Dothan, Alabama, where the highway expanded to four lanes again. From Dothan to Marianna was 35 miles, the last half of it again on the two-lane, macadam highways he was to grow used to in the Deep South.

The houses along the side of the road had just begun to grow closer together and more familiar, convincing him that he was finally at his destination when, in the rear-view mirror, he saw the flashing red of a police warning light and heard the muted growl of its siren.

He slowed and pulled to the side of the road, wondering what was wrong. The police car, a new, high-powered Dodge, pulled up beside him, and a highway patrolman in a wide-brimmed hat who didn't look much older than Dave leaned across the seat to call, "Y'all follow me, hear?"

"Yes, sir," Dave said.

Somewhat disturbed, and reflecting that he had had more trouble with the police in the last two days than he had ever before had in his life, he let out the clutch and dutifully followed the patrol car.

The road through town had been rebuilt since he had last been there (five years before) and was now six lanes wide and lined with new business buildings, including a shopping center and several automobile dealerships.

The police car's turn signals flashed brightly and the patrol car turned off the main road and into one of the automobile dealerships. At just about the same moment he saw six foot high letters reading KERR MOTORS, he saw Uncle Comer, all six feet four of him, coming through a plate-glass door in the plate-glass walls of the showroom.

He was wearing whipcord trousers, a well-washed, khaki shirt and a white, stockman's hat, as common in northern Florida as in Texas, Oklahoma and Montana.

"I was getting worried about you, boy," Uncle Comer said, "I put the law to looking for you."

"All in one piece, Comer," the Florida highway patrolman, now out of his car, said. He walked up to them as he hitched up his glossy leather belt and chrome plated .357 Magnum Smith and Wesson. "He was just ambling along the highway as if he knew the police were looking for him."

"I'm obliged to you," Uncle Comer said to the patrolman. "This is Chet Salles, Dave. I don't think you two have met before?"

"Not socially," Dave said, and the two men shook hands. "Thanks for the escort."

"We didn't want you lost, looking for the old place," Salles said. "And Comer was getting worried about you."

"Why?"

"Well, we heard what time you left Atlanta . . ."

"How did you hear that?" Dave asked.

"Well, I talked to your mother," Comer said, a little awkwardly, "and then I called up there to see if you needed anything. . . ."

"Oh," Dave said. He should be offended. He was perfectly capable of taking care of himself and did not need someone hovering over his every move. But Comer Kerr's affection was so shameless, so open, that it was impossible to be offended. He liked you, therefore he worried about you and tried to help you.

"We missed you from Atlanta to Columbus," the highway patrolman said, "but the Alabama Highway Patrol picked you up coming out of Phenix City, and then again coming out of Dothan. We knew when you crossed into Florida." He paused and smiled.

"You'd be surprised how easy it is to find, and then keep track of, a pizza truck towing a trailer," he added.

"I suppose," Dave said.

"Come on in. It's brand-new," Comer said, moving his hand in the general direction of the new building, "and I'm kind of proud of it."

He had reason to be proud of it, Dave decided, after they'd said good-bye to the highway patrolman and were inside the building. Not only was it new, but it was large and well planned. It was a two-sided building, with a glass walled showroom at each end. One of the showrooms was a tractor-and-farm-implement showroom. Cotton pickers and hay balers were on display in exactly the same luxurious surroundings as the most elegant of the passenger cars. To a farmer, Dave realized, a new and efficient farm implement is just as beautiful as a new and shining automobile.

The two showrooms were connected by the garage. Not only was it large, but it was a great deal more fully equipped than a garage of its size would have been up North. In a large city, few dealer-garages grind crankshafts, or for that matter, brake drums, because it is so much easier to take them to workshops which specialize in that kind of work. This was Marianna, Florida, not a big city.

As Dave got the conducted tour and shook hands with

fifteen or more mechanics whose names he was sure he would never remember, he saw that Comer was equipped to do practically anything but stamp out body panels. This garage could grind crankshafts and brake drums, and rebuild engines from the block up. There was massive, frame-straightening equipment, and a paint room equipped with water-washed air and an infra-red drying tunnel. They stood watching for five minutes while a great yellow school-bus body was lowered into place and then bolted on a chassis.

"It seemed kind of silly to either send the body from Texas to Atlanta for assembly at the truck-assembly plant, or send the bodyless truck to Texas. We're just about in the middle. We may come out all right, too, so far as the money goes."

"I'm impressed, Uncle Comer," Dave said. "Really impressed."

"Pete O'Hara tells me that you call him Pete," Comer said. "Now is there any good reason why you shouldn't call me Comer?"

"I guess not, if you want me to."

"I'd like you to," Comer Kerr said. "But I suspect that your aunt Marge would just as soon be called Aunt Marge."

"Yes, sir," Dave said.

"And I'm under orders to bring you over to the house as soon as you get here," Comer said. "So I suppose we'd better go."

"Yes, sir."

Dave thought it characteristic of Uncle Comer that Comer tossed Dave's luggage into a dusty pickup truck, despite the obvious fact that he could have taken, if not one of the half-dozen, shining, new cars from the passenger car showroom, then any of the one hundred or so cars on the used car lot. In Marianna, Comer didn't need a new car to remind people that he was the owner of Kerr Motors.

They didn't go toward the house, but Dave, curious to see the town again after the major road-building project, didn't say anything until they stopped before the vintage brick building whose windows bore obviously new lettering: KERR FEED AND SEED. The old lettering, put there by Dave's grandfather and Comer's father had read, COMER BRAGG KERR FEED, SEED, FERTILIZERS, FARM IMPLEMENTS, TRACTORS, TRUCKS & AUTOMOBILES.

"What are we doing here?"

"I want your professional judgment on something," Comer said.

"Oh?"

"Pete tells me that you're something of an expert," Comer said, and walked through the small door in the larger wooden doors to what had been the garage. Most of the area was now stacked to the rafters with bags of seed, feed, and a dozen varieties of fertilizer in neat, light-brown paper bags.

At the far end of the garage, under a tarpaulin, was an automobile. With a quick gesture of his massive wrists, Comer flipped the tarpaulin off. It was what Dave thought of as a dirt-track racer.

"Engine's shot," Comer said. "But the rubber's all right, and she's never really been wrecked."

"What are you doing with it?" Dave asked, without really thinking.

"Well, the truth of the matter is, I own it," Comer said, somewhat embarrassed.

"What for?"

"Well, I got a good price on it, Dave. And what I was thinking was that if you were willing to help me set it up for racing, I could sort of use it for advertising. There's a couple of little tracks around here. And advertising's the thing."

Dave understood all at once. Comer was being Comer. Pete O'Hara had told him that Dave wanted to flex his wings as a fledgling automobile racer. If that's what Dave wanted, that's what Dave could have. Comer had gone out and bought what he thought Dave wanted.

It was the last thing Dave wanted. Quarter-mile dirt track racing was a quick route to nowhere. It was expensive, there was never enough in prize money to do more than pay the expenses of the winner, and you couldn't use a quarter-mile dirt racer on the larger tracks.

But he couldn't tell Comer this. He couldn't hurt Comer's feelings.

He went to the car, a 1950 Ford coupe, and pulled open the hood. The engine was not only shot, it was missing. But the engine mounts appeared to be in good shape, and with a little effort, he could mount one of the spare engines from the Motor Enterprises Special in it. The car wasn't worth the engine, but it was a small price to pay for having an uncle like Comer Kerr.

"Not bad," he said. "One of my engines'll fit it."

"You like it, do you?" Comer asked.

"Yes, sir," Dave said. "That's quite a car."

"I wouldn't admit this to many people," Comer Kerr said, as he flipped the tarpaulin back in place, "but the truth is I don't know so much about these things as my reputation would have people believe."

"What did you pay for it?"

"Not much. About five hundred."

Dave knew that was two hundred too much at home, and that meant it was probably three hundred too much down here.

"For a car in that shape," Dave said. "You didn't do bad."

Comer beamed. Then said, "We'd better get moving. Marge'll eat us alive."

The Kerr home was a rambling, difficult-to-describe building on the outskirts of town. It was old and new. The place had originally been the Kerr farm, and the house the farmhouse. The word plantation was used then as it was used now, and it was used properly, even if the Kerr home was not a white, ante-bellum mansion with soaring pillars. A plantation was a place where things were planted. Great-grandfather Kerr had decided that he could make a little extra money by going into the feed and seed business. Additions were made to the barns then, and then to the house itself, as office space was required. Grandfather Kerr had made further additions, and so had Comer Kerr. The original farmhouse was still there, but it was difficult to tell exactly where. The barn complex was down to two barns now, two hundred yards from the house. Most of the cotton lands were in long-needle pine trees, and the farming operation wasn't very much.

The word that came to Dave's mind when he saw the place again was comfortable. It was a comfortable place. The rooms were large with high ceilings. The furniture was made and arranged to be used. There was a dining room which was used, and not saved for Thanksgiving or other appropriate occasions. The kitchen was a place to work, properly equipped with proper tools. Bedrooms were large and airy.

In the parking area near the kitchen were a brand-new station wagon, with the dealer's tag identifying it as the car Comer had set aside for Aunt Marge to use, a tractor hitched to a flat-bed, rubber-tired wagon, and a 1933 Ford station wagon.

At the age of eleven, Dave Wade had learned to drive in that station wagon. He had been turned loose in a field and told to try to avoid hitting a tree or the fences that bordered the field. He had succeeded, but his mother and Aunt Marge had been a chorus of outraged maternalism when Uncle Comer returned him to the house to boast of the new accomplishment.

"It's still running, huh?" he said.

"District manager said he'd give me a thousand dollars

for it," Comer said, "and then pay whatever I wanted to re-store it, to use it for an advertisement."

"You didn't agree?"

"Be like selling you, Dave," Comer said. "I don't think the wagon would last long if it had to leave the farm."

Dave sensed that Comer meant this, that he wasn't just saying it to earn a chuckle. And, having recently parted with the Stud-illac, he understood this completely.

By the time they turned off the engine and Comer had beat him to the cargo compartment of the pickup truck to snatch the heavy bags up as if they were empty, Aunt Marge was out of the house, across the porch, and down the shallow flight of stairs. She wrapped her arms around him, not sure, apparently, whether she was pleased with him or furious.

"Where've you been?"

"We went down to the old store," Dave said.

"I was afraid you weren't going to make it," she said, pushing Dave away from her now and looking up at him.

"I've been out here once or twice before," David Wade said. "I remembered the way pretty well."

"I mean in time for tonight," she said, "and you know it."

"Dave's had a long, hot drive," Comer said, going up the stairs to the porch, "and I suggest you give him something cold to drink and a place to sit down before you spring that on him."

"I didn't think," she said, and she took his arm and pro-pelled him into the house. Inside the door, he was wrapped inside thick, chocolate-colored arms.

"Lord, if you get any bigger, the house won't hold you and Comer too," she said. She was legally Mrs. Lester Crawley, owner, among other things, of some 2,200 acres of rich north Florida land. She was the guiding light of the Crawley Crossroads Baptist Church, and she was listed as a director of two insurance companies and one savings and loan institution.

She was known throughout the area as Aunt Leslie, which was her christian name, and she had been employed on the Kerr plantation for forty of her sixty years. She had been born on the Kerr plantation, and had married on the Kerr plantation. After a childless marriage of twenty years had left her a widow, she had returned to the Kerr plantation, her ample estate notwithstanding. She and her family were as much a part of the Kerr plantation as Comer and Marge Kerr, and she had come home. She had known Dave Wade all his life and took very much the same maternalistic pride in him as Marge Kerr did.

Aunt Leslie Crawley took him by the arm and led him into the kitchen. As she put a deep, white bowl of strawberries and cream before him, she demanded to know the complete details concerning his mother's health (for she had watched Dave's mother grow from an infant, and had watched when his mother went off and married that Yankee pilot) and that of his half-brothers and half-sister.

Dave's reaction to his reception was simply that it is rather embarrassing for a young man to be beamed upon by two obviously, even shamelessly, fond-of-him women in their middle years. He felt that he had been figuratively patted on the head, pinched on the cheek, and told that he was a nice, little boy.

"Now, what were you so afraid I was going to be late for?" he demanded. The two women looked at each other.

"I told your mama," Aunt Leslie said, "that we'd call the minute you got here." She got to her feet, waddled across the large, old-fashioned kitchen, and returned with an incongruously modern princess telephone on a long cord. She dialed the operator and gave Dave's mother's number from memory.

There was the muted sound of the telephone ringing and then something unintelligible, and then Aunt Leslie said, "Sitting right in front of me, Grace, eating strawberries and cream."

He spoke with his mother and with the children and felt very much like a child himself, again firmly in the grasp of a family, and then he passed the telephone to Aunt Marge. He concentrated on the strawberries, not paying much attention, and then he suddenly grew alert.

"I wish you were here to help, Grace. We've got all the nice, young people in town coming to meet him, and it's only Aunt Leslie and me to do the work."

His mother's voice, but not so clearly that he could understand what she was saying, said something, and then Aunt Marge laughed and said, "Well, I don't know. You got married in a hurry, and I got married in a hurry. But if it looks dangerous, I'll call again and you and Pete can come down on a plane in time for the ceremony."

Aunt Leslie laughed heartily, and Dave actively disliked her. When the call was over, he said, "Now what happens tonight?"

"We're having a little party for you," Aunt Leslie said. "Been working on it all day."

"I feel like a piece of merchandise out on display," he said.

"I don't think I'd put it quite that way," Aunt Marge said, a little hurt, so that Dave was suddenly ashamed of himself.

"I'm sorry I said that," he said. "But I guess I didn't appreciate the business about getting married."

"She's determined that we don't lose any more members of the family to the Yankees," Aunt Leslie said.

"Have you got something against marriage?" Aunt Marge asked.

"I think marriage is a fine and noble institution. I think everybody who has a job and the money and is prepared to support a wife should consider marriage. There is only one flaw in your reasoning. My total cash assets are a pizza truck, a wrecked racing car, two spare engines, and about ninety-seven dollars in cash."

"Why, Honey," Aunt Marge said. "If you need money, all you got to do is open your mouth. We're going to leave all this to you. I thought you knew that. I thought your mother told you. We told her."

He couldn't think of a thing in the world to say to that, so he stood up, looked down at the two women, and announced that he thought he'd better be taking a shower.

Five

UNCLE COMER, obviously ill at ease, came to Dave's room while he was shaving. This made Dave feel even more ill at ease, because he knew that there was no reason in the world to be offended, or for Uncle Comer to come trying to spread oil on the waters.

Comer was half dressed. That is, he had finished his shave, and the whipcord trousers had been replaced with the trousers to a cord suit. But he wore only his undershirt, and Dave sensed that Comer had decided, in the midst of dressing, that he would talk to Dave.

"I guess I'm at fault," he said. "Stick pins in me."

"At fault for what?"

"I could have stopped this party business when first I heard about it."

"I'm pleased."

"You're pleased like the little boy who says 'thank you' politely to the dentist," Comer said. "And I can't say I blame you. I suppose that we are putting you on display, and when I look at it from your side, I guess I'd be sore, too."

"I guess I was pretty rude," Dave said. "I didn't mean to be. I'll go tell her I'm sorry."

"You weren't rude. Under the circumstances, I'd say you were a southern gentleman, suh," Comer said, thickening his accent to make a little joke of the phrase. "It's not hard for me to figure out. What we've got here is two middle aged women . . . I guess you'd really have to call Aunt Leslie elderly . . . who have nothing much to do with their time but watch the sun come up and go down. You've got to remember that neither of them had children. That does something to a woman. What they've got is you, Dave. They can show you off. You're sort of a stand-in for the real thing."

"I hadn't thought about that," Dave said frankly. "It's just that I've never liked being in the middle. Some guys love it. But when I'm the center of attraction, I just sit there and feel ridiculous."

"Me, too," Comer admitted, and Dave knew he meant this.

"Something must be wrong with me," Dave said. "I should be very pleased and flattered."

"Nope," Comer said. "I don't think I'd like you so much if you were."

Dave chuckled.

"Tell you what," Comer said, "make like you're having a good time tonight, and I firmly guarantee that I will keep it from happening . . . I was about to say again, and I can't really promise that . . . I'll keep it from happening often. How's that for a deal?"

"I'm sure I'll have a good time," Dave said.

"Bravely said," Comer said. "Just like the little boy on his way to the dentist's office."

They both laughed, and then Comer grew serious again.

"About this place, Dave, and the business."

"Yes, sir?"

"I'm sorry your mother didn't tell you what we planned for it."

"I don't know what to say about it."

"Don't say anything yet," Comer said. "But will you tell me something?"

"Yes, sir."

"Are you really a competent mechanic, or is Pete sort of biased?"

"I think I am," Dave said. "You wanted an honest answer? I'm a very good mechanic. I've got a real feeling for it. Primarily for engines."

"O.K., that'll make it easier when I put you to work in the garage. One more thing, what kind of a driver are you? A race driver, I mean? I know just enough about that business to know that it's a tough one."

"I don't really know."

"What do you think?"

"You'll think I've got a swelled head," Dave said. "But I think I'm good."

"Are you safe?"

"Yes, sir."

"I don't want to wipe you off our tracks down here," Comer said.

"I'm cautious, too," Dave said.

"O.K.," Comer said. He stood up. For some reason, it seemed perfectly natural that they shake hands. They did so, and then Comer went out of Dave's room and down the corridor.

What Comer had said about the childless women made sense. But it also applied to childless men. The least he could do, he realized, was to put himself on display as Comer's nephew, as well. He had planned to wear a sport coat and a pair of slacks. Now he took his one good suit from the closet, and his good pair of shoes, and a brand-new shirt.

It wasn't as difficult as he thought (or, he admitted, as he could have made it by being determined not to have a good time). He knew many of the people from previous visits, although he remembered them only vaguely. They all seemed to have passed from childhood to near maturity since he had last seen them.

And, of course, under Aunt Leslie, it was a good party. She was a marvelous cook. The table held just about everything but southern fried chicken, and he thought of Pete O'Hara's remark that southern fried chicken was what the South had used to gain revenge for having lost the Civil War. They fed it only to Yankees. When he thought about it, he could not remember ever having eaten chicken in Florida. There was a roast turkey, and a baked ham, and plates of freshly cooked vegetables and heaping bowls of fresh rolls.

It was awkward meeting men he had not met before. They eyed him curiously, as if they expected him to shoot sparks out of his ears, or to stir his coffee with a fork, or otherwise demonstrate Yankee behavior. After three-quarters of an hour, he fled from the living room and library when a large, open-faced young man named Ray T. Lott, whom he remembered as a short, skinny, timid boy, asked if the old station wagon was still around.

Showing it to him and to one or two of the others gave him the excuse he needed to leave what was sort of a reception line. And once they were out there, it was easy to stay. First, of course, the engine had to be examined, and then it had to be started and listened to, and then shut off again, and examined again.

One or two of the girls came out after the boys, and he had just told himself that he was over the hump, that from here on in it would be coasting, and very likely even fun, when Aunt Leslie came out into the yard after him.

Her dress indicated that the party was an occasion of the first magnitude. She was wearing what Comer called her dress of many colors and her earrings. The earrings were the key. They were worn only on solemn, sad occasions (when her dress was black velvet) or at weddings, christenings, and the like, with the dress of many colors.

"You better get in the house," she ordered. "You can play with that smelly old wagon anytime. Your aunt's got some people she wants you to meet."

He was herded into the house through the kitchen with

Aunt Leslie's heavy, firm fingers on his arm as if to prevent flight.

"Here he is," Aunt Leslie announced loudly. "He was out messing with that old station wagon."

"Honey, I didn't mean to take you from your friends," Aunt Marge said. "But I did want you to meet these people. I went to school with her mother and with his mother. I don't know how you've missed meeting each other before when you were here."

"Oh, we've met," Dave said, putting out his hand. "Hello, Rufus. Nice to see you again."

"And do you know Anne, too?" Aunt Marge said, surprised.

"We have a nodding acquaintance," Dave said, putting out his hand to take the hand of the blonde he'd stared at at the race track in Atlanta. Her hand was every bit as warm and soft as he knew it would be, and her eyes were laughing, and he knew with an entirely delightful sureness that she was laughing with him, not at him, and that they were both laughing at Rufus, who took a good thirty seconds to close his mouth.

"Where's your pizza wagon?" Rufus finally said.

"Down at the garage," Dave said.

"Are you in . . . that . . . uh . . . business?" the blonde, Anne—what a pretty name—asked.

"No," he said.

"Just what do you do?" Rufus asked.

"I'm a mechanic, and I hope to enter racing."

"That's fascinating," Rufus said. "I race a little myself.

As a matter of fact, I'm racing next Friday. Have you got a car?"

"Yes, but it's wrecked."

"What have you got?" Rufus demanded, but politely.

" '61 Ford."

"Did you wreck it?"

"I wasn't driving."

"I don't suppose you'd be ready to race by next Friday?"

"Not in that car," Dave replied. "What sort of a track is it?"

"Half-mile, dirt. Pretty rough, unless you're used to it. And then you have to have a license."

"What kind of a license?"

"I don't suppose you've got a NASCAR license?"

"As a matter of fact, I do," Dave said. At that moment, Comer walked up.

"Excuse me," he said. "Did your aunt Marge find you?"

"Yes, sir. She wanted me to meet Rufus and Anne here."

"How are you, Rufus? We don't see you much anymore."

"Rufus has asked me to race," Dave said. "Do you suppose we could get an engine into that Ford by Friday."

"An engine, sure," Comer said, and he sounded disappointed. "But you just can't put any old engine in a car. . . ."

"I brought along a rebuilt engine that'll fit that Ford," Dave said, "all ready to race."

"In that case," Comer said, "there shouldn't be any problem at all."

It was entirely gratifying to be able to challenge Rufus Bowers, but even as the challenge was made and accepted, Dave had second thoughts. For one thing, he didn't have much racing experience at all, and almost none on half-mile dirt tracks. Moreover, what little experience he had was in the Motor Enterprises Special, a big, highspeed vehicle, not in a 1950 Ford, which probably wouldn't get out of second gear, on a half-mile dirt track.

He thought that there was a good chance, having mounted on the white charger to do battle for the hand of the fair maiden, that the stallion would run away with him, or that, even less glamorously, he would very likely fall off the horse.

In the morning, when they went down to Kerr Motors, the pizza wagon and the shrouded Motor Enterprises Special were inside the garage, parked in the center of it. What had happened was obvious. No one knew what to do with them.

"I thought that what we'd do, Dave," Comer said, "would be to haul this car down to the old place. And you could work there, if that would be all right?"

"Fine, thank you," Dave said.

"That way, you'll be free to do for you, and not be bothered all the time," Comer said, as if talking himself into it.

"That's perfect," Dave said.

"Well, come along, then," Comer said, "and we'll introduce you to the people we might have missed yesterday."

Dave was sensitive to the fact that he was being introduced as sort of the boss's son. All the jokes he had ever heard about nepotism ran through his mind.

"The boss's favorite nephew may not always be right, but he's always the boss's favorite nephew."

At the engine rebuild stand a mechanic in his middle thirties was torquing headbolts on a truck engine.

"Charley, this is Dave Wade," Comer said.

"Howdy," Charley said. "I'd shake hands, but mine are greasy."

He was friendly, but suspicious.

"You pretty well tied up, Charley?" Comer asked.

"Not too bad. Another thirty minutes or so on this, and I'll be loose. Something you want me to do?"

"You know that ol' 50 Ford I bought?"

"Yes, sir."

"Dave's going to race it next Friday."

"There's no engine," Charley said, matter of factly.

"Dave's got an engine," Comer said. "Can you help him put it in?"

"Sure. Soon's I'm finished here. You gonna bring it up here?"

"I thought you would work better in the old place."

"Whatever you say."

It had been friendly and polite, but what it really was, Dave knew, was that the boss had ordered a mechanic to do something that really had nothing whatever to do with Kerr Motors.

Comer left Dave with Charley and for a good ten minutes Charley worked in absolute silence on the truck engine bolting the generator in place, replacing carburetor on the intake manifold, hooking up the fuel lines.

"What kind of an engine you got for that old Ford?" he asked finally, softly, and so suddenly that he startled Dave.

"A sixty-one 380-cubic inch," Dave said.

"Good shape?" Charley asked, after a long pause.

"Just rebuilt," Dave said.

"Had it on a dynamometer?"

"No."

"Why not?"

"Haven't had a dynamometer," Dave answered.

"We got one here," Charley said and then grunted. Dave looked to see why he grunted. He had leaned heavily on a wrench. "Would you think it would be a good idea to put it on the dynamometer?"

"Sure," Dave said.

"Then let's us do that before we try to get it into that old Ford. Save us taking it out again later maybe."

"Sure."

"Where's the engine?"

"In the pizza wagon."

"You got it on a skid?"

"Yes, sir."

"Don't call me sir" Charley said. "Call me Charley."

"Call me Dave."

"O.K."

There followed another full three minutes of silence, then Charley said, "I saw that wrecked '61. Took the cover off and looked at it."

Dave didn't reply.

"You wrap it up like that?" Charley asked.

"No. Another fellow did."

"Looks like it could be rebuilt." Charley said.

"Yes, I think so."

"You planning to?"

"Yes, I think so."

There was no response to this, either. When Dave looked at the truck engine, he was surprised to see that everything was in place, that Charley at that moment was snapping the ignition harness to the spark-plug caps. He got inside the truck, and Dave saw the throttle mechanism work once or twice, and then Charley hit the ignition. After fifteen seconds of cranking, the engine started. Charley let it run for a moment, and then, without a word to Dave, backed the truck out of the bay, and down the center aisle, and then into a bay marked with an illuminated sign: TUNE UP.

Then he walked back, wiping his hands on a red grease rag.

"Let's have a look at this engine," he said. Dave found himself trailing after Charley like a dog following his master.

It took Charley less than fifteen minutes to connect the engine to the dynamometer. He worked with deceptive speed. It looked as if he were working very slowly, not unlike a slow motion film, but Dave saw that he never had to do one motion twice. Actually, Charley was as fast a mechanic as Dave had ever seen.

"Do you know how these work?" he asked, softly, nodding his head at the elaborate, and obviously new device.

"Yes," Dave said.

"O.K.," Charley said. "Let's see what it does."

He threw a switch, and the starter whined for a second, and then the engine caught, its exhaust muffled so well that it was uncannily quiet. Charley waited patiently until the manifold temperature-gauge indicator wiggled, and then came to life and moved up on the dial. Then he began to test the engine at various loads and throttle settings and carburetion adjustments. It took him a half-hour, and the only sound he made in that time was a noncommittal grunt.

Finally, he shut the engine down and turned to Dave.

"That one's O.K. Most people don't know what they're doing when they rebuild an engine. The guy that rebuilt that for you was a mechanic."

"I rebuilt that engine," Dave said.

Charley looked at him for a long minute, and then, as if thinking aloud, said, "Comer's a pretty good mechanic too, when he's got the time to do it." He paused again. "Let's go get us a cup of coffee while that cools down enough for us to unhook it."

Dave knew that he had been inspected and found passable.

Six

IT WASN'T much of a track. It was egg-shaped, a quarter-mile on each side, sloping gently toward the larger end. Going around, you would come out of the sharper turn and go downhill to the wider turn. The terms were relative. Both turns were sharp, and there really wasn't much of a slope.

On one straightaway, there was a grandstand. It could not have held more than 1000 people. Surrounding the rest of the track was the parking lot, separated from the track itself by discarded railroad ties buried in the ground and cemented there with concrete and heavy cables. There were two breaks in this barrier: one giving access to the paddock and pits; the second giving access only to the track. This was for the use of the ambulance and the wreckers.

The problem faced at other tracks of unauthorized people getting out of the paddock and into the pits was solved simply here. Unless you were racing or on the pit crew or an official, you did not enter the paddock at all. In that sense, there was no paddock. Inside the track was all pit.

The start-finish line was in front of the grandstand, and the officials were housed in a glass-windowed box sitting high above the track on steel stilts.

The place had been depressing when Dave Wade had first seen it as soon as they had installed the engine in the old Ford. It had needed a road test, and it was logical that it be tested where it would run, so they pulled the Motor Enterprises Special off the trailer, pushed what had come to be known as the old Ford onto it, and the pizza wagon had hauled it over to the track.

The road test told Dave several things. First, the track was rough. It was so rough that vibration would go beyond being an annoyance and would become a genuine problem. He'd have to beef up the springs and do something about the shocks. Because it was so rough, and because it was so short, the top speed of a car would not be at all important. He didn't think they'd have average running speeds of 70. Lap times would be closer to 50, with speed peaks not much over 70.

He was used to running laps of 75 and 80, with peaks of 100. He knew there would have to be some difference in racing technique, and wondered again if he had mounted the white charger only to fall flat on his face.

The rebuilt engine gave him all the torque he would need at the speeds at which he would be racing. The weak link in the power-transmission chain was second gear. That would have to be changed, and he would have to have, he decided, larger tires in the rear than the old Ford had mounted.

The track looked small and dismal on his second trip around it, the next day, with beefed up shocks and tied down springs and a new second gear and 10:00 by 16's in the rear.

And it looked dismal now, on Friday night, racing night, as he drove the pizza wagon through the lines of spectators' cars. There were more people present than he would have thought, and he was aware that at least three of them thought the pizza wagon was the funniest thing they'd seen since Henry Ford got out of the bicycle business.

Charley was waiting for him in the pits, once he'd bounced and lurched across the track again. Charley was not visibly moved, one way or the other, by his new role as chief mechanic. Dave wondered if Charley really wouldn't rather have been at home watching television or playing with his kids. There was a good chance that he had volunteered to be chief mechanic in the pits because Dave was the boss's nephew.

The boss, Uncle Comer, had announced that he would be in the way in the pits and would watch the races from the grandstand. Aunt Marge would not watch the races at all, and Dave could see that there was some problem there too. It was not difficult to imagine Aunt Marge prevailing upon Comer to prevail upon Dave to give up racing because she thought it was dangerous, unprofitable, and unfitting.

He never quite understood what unfitting meant, but it was a word both his aunt Marge and his mother used frequently. The first two points had some inarguable merit.

There was a certain amount of danger. Accidents did

happen. People even got killed. More people got injured. If it had not been for a broken leg and a spectacular crash, for example, he wouldn't even be the sole proprietor of Motor Enterprises, Inc., and in Florida.

What Pete O'Hara would call the profit picture wasn't exactly bright, viewed with objective eyes. He had made up his mind to pay Uncle Comer for Charley's time, and had found out, with some effort, that this meant he would have to pay for eighteen hours of work at $3.25 an hour. That was $58.50. The tires, even wholesale, were a $100. Adding that to the entrance fee, his insurance, and the other small costs, he had invested more than $250 before running his first race. And that did not take into consideration the cost of the old Ford, the cost of rebuilding the engine.

The track paid $2.50 lap money. He didn't think he'd get any of that, because people who took lap money usually had very fast cars and a bland attitude toward burning them out. In the major race, the top spot paid $250. Second place paid $100, and third $50. There were two smaller races with prizes of $150, $75 and $25. There was a novice race, which he would have to enter to comply with track regulations. This meant that he would have to race his investment against prizes of $25, $10 and $5. And there was a qualifying race paying $100 and $50, with no third prize. Only the top ten contenders in the qualifying race were permitted to enter the major race.

There were obviously a large number of drivers competing for the prize money, drivers with more general experience, more experience on dirt tracks, and more experience on this dirt track behind the wheel of dirt-track racers.

All he had, Dave realized, as he and Charley pushed the old Ford off the trailer onto the track, was a good engine, good rubber, and a driver with a large mouth.

Charley slipped behind the wheel of the old Ford and brought the engine to life, warming it slowly and carefully, checking the oil pressure and the water and manifold temperatures.

The safety inspector came around while Dave was slipping into the borax-smelling coveralls. He ran an experienced eye over the brake lines and the fuel lines, and gave the roll-bar a healthy push and pull. He sniffed Dave's coveralls and asked for his license. He checked it against the NASCAR and USAC lists of disqualified drivers, and then shook Dave's hand and wished him well.

"It's warm," Charley said and got out of the car. Dave got in, slipping on a pair of thin, leather gloves at the last minute. He slid the seat back and forth nervously until he got it just where he wanted it. Then he took a crescent wrench from Charley and bolted the seat firmly in place. He pulled the shoulder harness to his lap, connected it with the seat belt, and drew both tight. Charley handed him his helmet, and he buckled it on. There was nothing left to do.

He nodded at Charley, dropped the lever into low, tapped the accelerator, let out the clutch, and moved along the pits toward the start-finish line.

The loudspeaker blasted in his ear.

"Moving up to the starting line for a trial lap is Number Seventy One, a nineteen fifty Ford powered by a sixty-one

380-inch engine. Driver is the owner, Wade Davis."

The announcer was loud and incorrect, Dave thought.

An official in a striped black and white shirt waved the flag at him, and he let out the clutch and hit the accelerator.

At least, he thought, as he upshifted into second and let his eyes drop to the tachometer, when I fall flat on my face, "Wade Davis" will fall flat on his face, and Dave Wade's reputation will be intact.

He experimented with the gears in the turn and decided that he was right, that using third would be foolish. What would win here would be powered slides around these turns, and that required torque more than anything else. His torque would be in second.

He took four laps, including one he thought was a good, fast one. Then he got the flag to leave the course; the races were about to start. As he slowed and turned off, he could hear the loud-speakers. He had made, during what he was sure was a fast lap, a speed of 53.125. That was about five miles slower than he thought he was going.

Charley said nothing when he stopped at the pits and un-strapped himself. He raised his eyebrows questioningly. Dave replied with the O.K. sign.

The first race was the opener, one of the two 20-lappers paying $150, $75, and $25. There were fifteen contenders and Dave was barred from entering until he had raced in the novice class and been judged safe.

He was just as glad, for this would give him a chance to study the opposition.

He had just finished telling himself this when he faced the

reality. He knew as little about what made a good dirt-track racer as anyone in the stands. He was racing in the novice race because he was a novice.

Rufus went by, driving a '52 Chevrolet. The body work was badly banged up, but the engine sounded properly tuned, and the exhaust showed little black smoke. The tires, Dave saw, were new, or nearly new. Rufus was not the sort who would risk his neck on cheap tires. Rufus waved at him, and Dave waved back. Someone who didn't know them would have thought them the best of friends.

It's funny, Dave thought, with the exception of that exchange of remarks in Atlanta, there have been nothing but courtesies exchanged between us, and yet we both seem to have admitted that we don't like each other. Was that because of the girl, Anne, or would they have disliked each other if there had been no blue-eyed blonde?

When the flag went down, it sounded like so many explosions, and there was a low-hanging cloud made up of exhaust fumes, scorched rubber, and pulverized dirt from the track.

They went into a bunch at the first turn, and there was a sound of rending metal and screaming rubber, and two cars bounced off the railroad ties and across the track and then coasted ignobly to a stop.

Pit crews rushed onto the track and pushed them out of the way. On a half-mile track, there isn't much time between laps.

He watched the action carefully with a sincere interest, but he really wasn't sure that Number 11 had won until the loudspeakers announced this information, and he had no idea whatever who had taken second and third places.

What he did think, when he saw Number 11 take the victory lap with the checked flag held out the window was that the driver looked like a professional, and that there was a very good chance one David Wade was playing in the wrong league.

The novice race was next, and Dave was in the car buckling on the helmet again when he remembered that Rufus apparently hadn't placed in the first race. He hadn't even noticed him as the race ran its course.

Positions for the novice race were assigned alphabetically. And by this time, the officials had gotten his name right. He was David Wade, with a 'W.' The only car behind him on the starting grid was a '48 Ford marked The Young Special.

He felt uneasy in his stomach and considered this and faced the reason. He was afraid. You could get hurt racing. Looking around him, he could see that he wasn't the only one with a certain amount of fear. Three cars ahead of him a young face was green colored and covered with sweat.

There was a great deal of engine racing, crescendos of exploding, unmuffled exhausts, like a battery of machine guns or a string of large firecrackers. He could never see any real point in doing this. If it did blow out the carbon, then the engine was not in condition to race.

When the flag went down, it took Dave by surprise. The others were a good two heartbeats ahead of him. In the column of cars next to him, one over-anxious driver rammed the tail of the car ahead of him, and the two cars buckled in the middle.

Instinctively, Dave hit the brakes even as the shift lever went into second. And instinctively, as the buckling cars came into his lane, he whipped the wheel of the old Ford to the left. He felt it sag heavily on the right spring, and start to slide. He jammed his foot to the floor, breaking the slide, and then cut the wheel to the right again. He started to slide again and had to jam the accelerator again to keep from losing control.

The result of this violent maneuver was to whip him around the buckling cars. He had gone from behind them on the right, to parallel to them on the left, and when he was parallel to them he was still accelerating. It was a chance, he knew, but he kept his foot to the floor until the two sliding cars, still connected, were behind him. He was far, perhaps too far, into the turn now, but he had at least avoided the danger of being rammed should either or both of the cars swing back into the original path.

An old, old Ford, so battered and torn that he couldn't identify it any closer than a 1935–38, was into the corner, and pointed toward him. The driver panicked, hit the brakes, lost control, and slid to the outer edge of the track into the path of a '52 Oldsmobile coupe, who hit it square and then slid itself.

Dave was aware that he could not do anything but try to get around the turn without rolling or losing control of his four-wheel slide. He concentrated on doing that. And then he was out of the turn and on the tail of a '53 Chevie who was taking his half of the track right out of the middle.

With a wild feeling of exhultation at having missed the pile-up, Dave was content to stay in the Chevie's wake for the next complete lap. Out of the corner of his eye, he saw the ancient Ford coupe and the '52 Olds stopped against the railroad ties. The two cars which had buckled, forcing him to so violently change lanes, were apparently undamaged and probably somewhere on his tail.

Going into the narrow turn, Dave saw that the Chevie entered it wide, and took it wide and slow, and then recovered slowly. Dave had the wild idea that if he could pick up enough speed, he could cut under the Chevie's line on the wide turn, moving close to the retaining wall when the other car cut wide. If he could maintain his speed, he could pull ahead of the Chevie. Dave looked down at the tachometer. He had another 1000 rpm under his foot. He used it, pressing the wide, flat accelerator with his heel and toes.

The driver of the Chevie looked at him with surprise when Dave pulled parallel, and then corrected his path through the turn. For a moment, Dave was afraid that the left fender of the Chevie would catch his right door or right rear fender, but he went through the turn and into the straightaway and there was no crash, no sound of roaring metal, not even a bump.

He felt proud of himself until he saw how far behind he trailed the leaders of the pack, and how densely, as if they were wired together, they went around.

He closed the distance between them quickly, with a deep feeling of pleasure about the power of the engine, but he could not even enter the pack, much less pass even the trailing members of it, until at least five laps had gone by.

Resigned to not placing, he drove, nevertheless, as hard as he could, telling himself that he needed the experience. In three or four more laps, he had worked his way into the center of the pack. There were cars packed solidly behind his now, as well as in front.

If the pack was this far back, where were the leaders?

Finally, he broke through the pack, and could see the answer three-quarters of a lap ahead of him. He stood no chance whatever of catching them, and there were four of them. But, he decided, at least I might come in fifth. He drove fast now, but not quite as hard as he'd driven getting through the pack. He concentrated on cutting close to the barrier on the curves and in controlling his four-wheel slide as closely as possible.

And then he was coming around the narrow turn and into the stretch in front of the grandstand, to cross the start-finish line. There was apparently something wrong, the starter was out there in his black and white shirt, knees bent, about to give somebody the black flag, for he had the flag furled in his hand. And then, completely baffling Dave, the official jumped up in the air, and whipped the flag down at him, and it wasn't the black flag, it was the checkered flag, the winner's flag.

He was so startled that he turned and looked out the back window and saw that the official was pointing the checkered flag at another car behind him. He was still not sure of what was going on until he'd made one more lap, and this time the official was standing in the middle of the track, the checkered flag extended to Dave.

The loudspeaker said: "Winner of the novice race, in his first race at the Alafla track, David Wade, driving his own 1950 Ford. Official speed 52.185."

He blushed all the way around the track on the winner's lap.

When Dave got back to the pits, Charley finally had something to say, "You're pretty good at this, aren't you?"

"Beginner's luck," Dave replied, but he hadn't quite meant this. He had had a very uncomfortable feeling as he made the winner's lap, holding the checkered flag.

"Beginner's luck," was a good and satisfactory explanation for his having won. But he knew that it wasn't quite true, that it hadn't been beginner's luck. There had been an element of good fortune, certainly. But there had also been an engine that had delivered power when it was needed without hesitation. There had been tires with bite. And there had been a certain amount of physical skill on the part of the driver. He had known what he was doing when he'd whipped around the buckling cars at the very beginning of the race, and he had known (not guessed, or hoped, or dared) that he could make it around the turns as fast as he had made them.

He was unused to patting himself on the back, and he had fought these thoughts, telling himself that he would thereafter have a hard time getting his swollen head out of the crash helmet, that he would need less gas in the races in the future, because he could propel himself with his own hot air.

A race-course official came to the pits, wearing a bras-sard on his arm to identify himself.

"The race director," he began without any other prelimi-naries, "says you can enter the qualifying race, if you want to. You can run on this track from now on."

"Thank you," Dave said.

"You want to run in the qualifier?" the official asked. Dave nodded.

If he was blowing his own horn, if he really was a novice, if the confidence he had was nothing more than a personal pat on the back, there would be no better way to find out than by entering the qualifying race.

With the exception of Rufus, who obviously had some money (people normally do not ride around in brand new fire-engine red Thunderbirds when paying the rent is a problem), the other racers in the qualifying race needed to win, because winning meant money, and stock-car racing, even at the Alafla track, was no longer a hobby. It was much too expensive for a hobby.

"Why don't you go get a coke or something?" Charley asked. "Relax a little. I'll gas it up. And I think I'd better have a look at those plugs too."

Dave nodded his head in thanks. In his mind, he com-puted: 8 sparkplugs at $1.65 = $13.20. He had won $25.00 first place money, plus $12.50 in lap money (for the five laps he'd led) which made the gross income $37.50. From that he had to subtract his $10.00 entrance fee, the $5.00 car inspection fee, and the $13.20 for plugs. That was a total of $28.20, leaving a profit of $9.30.

That did not take into consideration, of course, wear and tear on the engine, on the tires, and what he owed Uncle Comer for Charley's services. Nor, of course, did it include the cost of the car, tires and fuel. By winning the novice race, he had cut his loss from nearly $300 to just over $250.00.

Seven

HE HAD TO WAIT for the track to clear before officials let him and twenty or thirty other drivers and mechanics cross over. He had taken off his racing coveralls, but he noticed that other drivers kept theirs on, or, if they had taken them off, had replaced them with shiny jackets on which their names were sewn.

He thought that this probably was one of the appeals of automobile racing. In a society where people more and more lost their identity and became simply numbers on the pay roll, racing cars provided an outlet for individuality.

People liked to watch it for that reason too. It was an open competition, and practically everyone could imagine himself taking the checkered flag for the winner's lap.

He ordered two hot dogs, all the way, and a coke from the refreshment stand, and had just taken a large, full, mouthful of hot dog, mustard, castup, roll, piccalilli, pickle, and chili when Anne spoke to him.

"You look deep in thought," she said and smiled.

His mother's voice came to him then, very clearly. "David, you eat as if someone's going to take it away from you. With your mouth stuffed like that, you look like the roast pig being taken before the king."

There was nothing whatever he could do but attempt the impossible, to chew quickly and yet have it appear that he wasn't chewing at all.

"Would you like a hot dog or a coke?" he asked, after a long painful period of enforced silence.

"The hot dogs look good," Anne said, and then, by blushing, she made it all too clear that she had noticed his stuffed mouth.

She turned from him and didn't look at him again until the hot dog and coke had been delivered.

"I came with Rufus," she said. "He's in the next qualifying race."

"I thought he was in the first one?"

"He was, but he didn't place," she said, and then, as if she had thought about it just then, "Congratulations. That's something to be proud of, winning your first race."

"Thank you," he said.

"Would you like to watch the qualifying race with me?" she asked.

"I'm running in it," he said.

"Oh?" she said, and she was surprised.

"Does that surprise you?"

"The way Rufus explained it, you would have to run in novice races until the race steward or the chairman decided you were good enough to race in . . . I guess with the others."

He didn't reply, and this, she soon saw, was a reply in itself.

"Oh," she said. "They've decided you can race."

"Yes."

"Are you sure you want to?"

"Why not? I might win. I need some of the money I've got invested back."

"Do you expect to win?" she asked, and her tone of voice somehow suggested that she was disappointed in him.

"I don't know. But there's only one way to find out," he said.

"Dave, this is a business to you, isn't it?" she asked.

"Yes, ma'am," he said.

"I never thought of it that way before," she said. "Rufus races for the fun, I suppose."

"He tries to get his money back, doesn't he?" Dave asked. Something about her attitude annoyed him; he could see nothing wrong with racing as a business.

"Yes."

"Then he's hardly a pure amateur, is he?" Dave said.

"No, I guess not," she admitted.

The loudspeaker interrupted the conversation, "The track will be cleared for five minutes to permit racing personnel, only, to return to the pits," the metallic voice said. "Five minutes only. After that, if you're out, you stay out. Five minutes only."

"I'll have to go," Dave said.

"Good luck," she said, and she smiled at him.

She doesn't think I stand a chance, Dave realized. Maybe she's right. Maybe I don't.

He knew something about how Pete O'Hara's mind worked. And he knew that Pete was the force behind his mother's decision to let him race. It was easy to imagine Pete deciding, and telling his mother, "Let him go. He won't last long. He'll realize that it's a rough, tough business, and not for him. Finding that out and then quitting is better than refusing him permission to race, which he would resent for a long, long time."

But all of a sudden all of the racing business, and the reasons behind it, and the possible future slipped from his mind. He found himself looking at the girl, and then he heard himself talking, "Are you and Rufus engaged or going steady or anything?"

"No," she said. "Not that it's really any of your business."

"I was going to ask you to go to a movie or something," he said.

"In the pizza wagon?" she asked.

"No, as a matter of fact, in a 1933 Ford station wagon," he said, a little angrily.

"I'd love to," she said.

"O.K.," he said, and now that it was all over, he was embarrassed and didn't know what else to say. "I'll call you."

Then he turned quickly away and trotted to the track. He was stopped at the barrier by an official who didn't recognize him. For a frightening two minutes he was unable to take Dave's word that he was about to race in the second qualifier.

"I can vouch for him," a vaguely familiar voice said. "I'm in his pit crew."

"Hello Roger," the official said. "I didn't see you before."

"I just got here," Roger Chedister said. "I may be too late. Have I still got a job in the pits, Dave?"

"Sure," Dave said, and the two shook hands.

"You-all better hurry," the official said, nodding toward the sound of the revving engines.

"What are you driving?" Roger asked, when they were out of earshot.

"A fifty Ford."

"They letting you run without running in the novice races?"

"I ran in the novice race."

"How'd you do?"

"I took it," Dave said simply.

"Lucky?" Chedister asked, as they came near Charley and the old Ford.

"A little, sure," Dave said.

"But a good car helps, huh? And knowing what you're doing?"

"Yes," Dave said, then, "Charley, this is a friend of mine, Roger Chedister. He's just joined the pit crew. Roger, this is Charley Kramer."

They shook hands.

"I'm not much good at engine work," Roger said. "And I don't know much about carburetors. But I bow to no man in wheel changing and tank filling."

Charley smiled, and Dave knew that Charley didn't smile at people he didn't like. Roger could make people like him soon after they met him. He wondered if Roger exercised this talent all the time or whether he used it only for people he had decided to like. Most of all, he wondered what Roger was doing here, whether he had sought Dave out, or whether the meeting at the barrier was just a coincidence. There was no time to dwell on the questions.

Dave had put on the coveralls again, the smell of borax now mingled with the smell of his own sweat and the mingled smells of burned rubber, gasoline, and lubricating oil.

Working as if he'd done it daily for months, Roger checked the seat for position and rigidity, gave the roll-bar healthy, knowing tugs and pushes, checked the tightness of the seat and shoulder straps and, with a lens tissue, cleaned Dave's goggles.

Then, he slapped Dave on the back and made Churchill's V for Victory sign with his fingers. In the car, Dave let the clutch out and moved out on the track. An official saw him and guided him to his spot on the starting grid.

There was no time to relax. The warning flag went up even as he pulled into position and shifted into neutral.

The cars against which he would be running now were better cars than those in the novice race. They were generally Fords and Chevrolets, and most of them were later models than Dave's 1950 coupe. Two cars looked out of place, a 1963 Oldsmobile, and a 1963 Pontiac.

Dave didn't know, in the sense that he couldn't prove it,

but, considering what cars in that class cost, and what the possible prize money was here at Alafla, he felt sure that the sleek sides concealed the marks of a bad wreck.

The owners and the drivers (probably owner-drivers, like himself) had decided that a totally wrecked big league car, unfit for further major track racing, and for sale cheap, could be put to work on the small, dirt tracks. The thinking was that enough of the original, pre-wreck, tremendous power and strength remained to outclass older cars, and those which had not been completely rebuilt.

It wasn't the first time Dave had seen cars like this. One look had convinced him that the owner-drivers were wrong, and that they could have better spent their money rebuilding older cars.

The flag went down. In the instant he saw it begin its downward movement Dave pulled the shift lever into low and let out on the clutch. He didn't stay long in first gear, for there was enough torque in second to carry the load.

He couldn't see very well or very much, for the cars bunched almost immediately heading into the first turn. But these weren't novices or learners. As if they were tied together, they slid into the turn, and then out of it, and picked up speed for the straightaway. There was a jockeying for position, but on a course of this size, with straightaways less than a quarter-mile long, there was neither the place nor the time for much of this.

Dave headed the nose of the old Ford close to the corner, and then was forced to ease up on the accelerator when a '54 Ford coupe's nose occupied the space first. In five laps, most of the cars were still bunched up, but the bunch had grown longer. It had changed shape from a bunch of grapes to a bunch of bananas.

This gave Dave an idea. It was obvious to him that they were going to go around and around without losing or gaining position unless something happened. An accident or a motor or power train failure would force a car out, and every car behind would move up one space.

There would be some battling for position when that happened and IF that happened, but Dave didn't think he was quite skillful enough to take the advantage of that situation.

He had one strength that he thought was both uncommon in the pack and unsuspected. Even with new gears in the rear end, his transmission-engine package gave him a greater top speed than he needed or was expected to have. If he went outside the pack, rode the edge, this would require that he travel at a faster speed. It would then be possible that he could pass many of the bunched cars, and possibly even get close enough to the head of the pack to take advantage when a car dropped out.

Deciding that he had nothing to lose, he began to slide to the right. He soon found that he would have to drop behind the car to his right in order to get around it. He accomplished this as they went around the next—the wider—turn.

He let the car slow as it began to slide, until the rubber regained traction. What had happened ran through his mind, like the electric sign in Times Square. AT POINT X, THE FORCE OF FRICTION BETWEEN THAT POR-

TION OF THE TIRE IN CONTACT WITH THE
TRACK AND THE TRACK ITSELF OVERCAME, THE
FORCES OF INERTIA. IN OTHER WORDS, THE
BODY IN MOVEMENT, HAVING BEEN ACTED
UPON BY AN OUTSIDE FORCE, NO LONGER RE-
MAINED IN ITS ORIGINAL PATH OF MOTION.

He was now in full control of the direction. He was also
now behind the car which had been next to him. He cut to
the right, slammed down on the accelerator, and then cut
sharply to the left again. He was in a two-wheel drift now,
just where he wanted to be. He cut the wheels right and left
again with a quick movement of his wrists, and he was out
of the drift, on the outside, with the tachometer indicating
that he could shift into high and pick up more speed. It had
worked.

Rather, it had partially worked. He knew now that he
could keep up with the bunched cars. Whether he could
pass them or improve his position was an entirely different
and unrelated matter. What little space he was able to gain
on the straightaway, he lost in the turns, for he had no
safety margin as a cushion against an unwise slide. If he
didn't slide where he intended to slide, he would slide into
the railroad ties.

And then the driver of a '63 Oldsmobile, one of the major track cars, one of those Dave felt sure had been
wrecked, saw what he was doing and repeated Dave's mo-
tions of going up to the rail on the outside. As Dave
watched, helpless to do anything about it, the Olds moved
in front of him. The gap the Olds had left in the pack was

promptly filled.

It was apparent that Dave had lost his gamble, that he hadn't been thinking nearly as cleverly as he had allowed himself to think he had. Instead of being alone on the outside, where he could take advantage of whatever developed, he was on the outside, boxed out by an Olds, and forced to eat the Olds' exhaust.

And that was more than a figure of speech. The Olds was laying a dust-colored cloud of dust and oil-fumes, and Dave could see scum form on the windshield of the old Ford. He was first annoyed, and then angry, and then he told himself that something was wrong with the Olds. It was throwing larger spots of oil, rather than half-burned oil which had passed through sloppy rings into the combustion chamber of the engine. In the instant his mind told him the Olds had an oil leak, there was a dull glow (not a flash and not a fire) and then the Olds began to lay a thick cloud of dense oil smoke.

It came from beneath the car, rather than from the engine, and Dave guessed that the oil was being blown back under the engine to some point below the driver, where it was striking the exhaust system. The driver, apparently not checking his rear-view mirror, was apparently unaware of what was happening.

The smoke itself seemed to roll toward the center of the track, and then was picked up by turbulent air at the front of the pack. The cars in the pack were getting the oil smoke, not Dave. He was getting unburned spots of oil, which were now splattering like light rain on the windshield.

The smoke had started just past the start-finish line and had grown thick as they entered the first turn. It hadn't grown any thicker, but neither had it slackened, as they traveled the rear straightaway. Then the pack began to slow.

There was a reason for this, too. As soon as the smoking car came to the attention of the officials, it would be black-flagged off the course. There was no sense in risking a pile-up, or a bad wreck going around the final turn, when the offending car would soon be tossed out of the race.

By now, Dave was sure that the driver of the Olds had seen the smoke. He remembered that it is difficult to see how much smoke is behind the car you're driving. In any event, the driver of the Olds seeing that he was pulling abreast and then ahead of the bunched cars, took advantage of the situation. He pulled from the rim, and took the lead by the inner rail.

Hot on his tail was the 1950 Ford driven by Dave Wade. He did this without considering what he was doing, other than to decide it wasn't dangerous, and he stood no chance of losing anything more than he had already lost. With the oil on the windshield, he would be blinded if he had to fol-low the pack again.

In the straightaway, there was another glow under the Olds, and then a flicker of flame.

The flagman was waving the black flag furiously. Dave thought, a quick idle thought, that if his hands were sweaty, and he lost his hold on the flag staff, he would throw it across the track and over the grandstands.

The Olds in front of Dave slowed and pulled suddenly off the track onto the pit apron. Dave had been in second. Leaving his right foot on the floor, he went up into high as he whipped the wheel to the right and left to get around the car.

Now he was leading and he knew it. Behind him, like so many angry hornets screaming in rage, the bunch set out after him. But they had lost too much time. By the time they finished jockeying for second, third, and fourth behind him, the race was practically over.

On the last turn into the final straightaway, the car in third place went way out and tried to make up in speed the greater distance to be traveled. He misjudged either the speed of his slide, or the distance to the railroad ties, or the adhesion of his tires, for he slammed into the ties broadside and bounced off them, out of control, narrowly missing the grouped cars.

The car in second place, a Chevie, took advantage of the gap left to pull abreast of Dave, and then tried to accelerate. He gained some speed, but not enough. He was still gaining when they crossed the finish line, but the checkered flag was waved at Car 71, a 1950 Ford, owner-driven by David Wade.

It wasn't until he'd taken the winner's lap and pulled into the pits that Dave saw that the second place driver was Rufus. He caught Rufus looking at him, and when Rufus saw him, he looked quickly away. There was no question that Rufus was angry about something, and when Dave wondered what it could be, the only answer was the race.

He then looked for the first time at Rufus' car and recognized it as the one which had pulled abreast of him, but hadn't had the power to pull ahead.

Charley, solemn, glum-faced Charley, was smiling from ear to ear. Roger Chedister had his arms folded on his chest as Dave coasted to a stop with the engine off.

"All it takes is a good pit crew," Chedister said as he handed Dave a coke bottle full of water. "Isn't that so, Charley?"

They laughed. Dave drained the water without taking the bottle from his lips.

"We'll have to keep you around, Roger," he said. "You're lucky."

"How'd it handle?" Charley asked, even as he went to the hood and raised it.

"Perfect," Dave said. "Couldn't ask for better. It went like a scared rabbit."

"How do you feel?" Chedister asked.

"Exhilarated," Dave said.

"Cocky?" Chedister asked.

"Not cocky," Dave answered. "There was a lot of luck in this."

"How do you mean?"

"Well, I was boxed on the outside by that Olds. If he hadn't developed oil trouble, I'd still be out there, unable to move."

Chedister nodded, and Dave sensed that Chedister hadn't needed to be told about how the race had been run and won; that what he wanted to know was whether the winner knew how it had been run and won. More specifically, Dave sensed that Chedister wanted to hear him admit that the major contributing factor to his victory was luck, coupled with a passable driving skill. Dave had not won because he was so good, but because he had had a good car and a lot of luck.

"Are you going to take the main event, Dave?" Roger asked innocently.

"Probably not."

"Are you going to try?"

"I'm going to try to place," Dave said. "Winning's something else."

"Why?"

"Because there are a lot of drivers out there who need to win this race more than I do," Dave said. "Many of them a whole lot better drivers."

"What about that business of racing to win?" Chedister challenged.

"I like that saying that goes 'Discretion is the better part of valor,' " Dave countered.

"Could we rephrase your position," Chedester asked, still not quite a joking, but not feeling serious, either, "to be that you 'will try to win, if you can win without taking foolish chances'?"

"Well said," Dave agreed.

"O.K.," Chedister said. He smiled and punched Dave in the arm. "They're going out on the grid," he said. "You'd better get back in the monster."

"Yes, sir."

Chedister repeated his professional, skilled, cockpit check, testing the seat belt, shoulder harness, the bolts holding the seat in place, and again cleaning Dave' goggles.

Dave pushed in the clutch, tapped the accelerator, and prepared to let out the clutch. Chedister held up a finger, and Dave let the engine die to an idle again.

"The drivers out there are more experienced than you," Chedister said. "But that doesn't make them necessarily better drivers."

"What's that supposed to mean?"

"It means that when you get more experience, Buddy, you're going to be really good," Chedister said, and then he stood erect and banged his fist on the roof of the old Ford, giving Dave the impression he was inside a steel drum. Then Chedister walked away from the car and jumped neatly over the railroad ties that formed the pit wall.

Dave let out the clutch and took his place on the starting grid.

_____ Eight

THE TALK about winning and placing turned out to be academic. Of eighteen starters, three cars had wrecked out. A right, front fender—left, rear fender encounter had taken a '60 Plymouth and a '61 Chrysler into the railroad ties and out of the race. Then one of the cars behind Dave (there were only two) had, without any obvious reason, gone out of control and spun out, smashing its rear against the railroad ties.

That left fifteen cars. Of these, four failed to finish. One broke an oil line and went smoking into the pits, two simply stopped running, and the fourth lost a right, rear wheel, including six inches of axle, and bounced to a stop on the far straightaway.

Eleven of the eighteen starters finished. The 1950 Ford owner-driven by David Wade finished ninth. He had managed, trying as hard as he knew how, to stay ahead of the one car behind him, and then, in the last three laps, to pass one of the nine cars ahead of him.

He knew he had managed this only because the three cars at the end were so far behind the others that he had been able to drift out from the rim toward the outside, and then overtake the car ahead of him with speed rather than skill.

As a race, it had been as frustrating as getting stuck in traffic.

He made the final turn, kicked the lever into neutral, let out the clutch, and reached forward to pull down on the toggle switch that, rather than the installed key lock, now controlled the ignition. The old Ford backfired once, as if reluctant to shut off, and died. He knew what the backfire was. It was gas being detonated by the heat of the combustion chamber. This is what he was thinking about as he turned the wheel slightly and stepped on the brake for the last time. He didn't even want to think about the race.

He unfastened his chin strap and then bent his head to unbuckle himself from the safety harness. He pulled off his gloves and saw that, despite them, his hands were filthy. They were sweat and oil soaked and caked with dried dust. When he spread them, white cracks of clean flesh appeared.

"You all right, Dave?" Chedister said, sticking his head inside the car, his voice concerned.

"I'm tired," Dave said and smiled.

"You look like you're made up for a minstrel show," Chedister said, chuckling.

Dave demonstrated a quickness of movement he didn't feel like making and got out of the car. Charley handed him the coke bottle full of water, and then Dave saw Uncle Comer come into the pits with a second man, similar in build and also, somehow, obviously southern.

"I've seen men clean grease sumps," Uncle Comer said, a faint smile on his face, "and look cleaner than you do."

"He got that oil from the Olds," the other man said. "But he's sure dirty, isn't he?"

"Dave, this is Lou Watters," Comer said. "Lou, my nephew Dave."

"How are you, Boy?" Lou Watters said.

"How do you do, sir?" Dave said. Lou Watters took, without hesitation, the greasy hand Dave automatically had put out, and then, remembering how dirty it was, pulled halfway back.

"You've met Roger Chedister?" Dave asked, "And Charley."

"I've known Charley since they brought him out of the woods and gave him his first pair of shoes," Watters said. "And I know Roger, sure enough."

Dave just smiled and waited. He knew that Watters wanted something, but he had no idea what.

"I got a track up in Bainbridge," Watters said, as if answering Dave's unspoken question. "I can see my way clear to giving you two-fifty starting money for Wednesday night. How's that strike you?"

"What kind of a track?" Dave asked, and he was afraid that he sounded rude. He was so tired.

"Three-quarter mile, banked turns, macadam," Watters said. "Deal?"

"How far is Bainbridge?" Dave asked, and he turned automatically to Roger to ask.

"About seventy-five miles," Roger answered.

"Will you go with me?" Dave asked. "You and Charley?"

Both men nodded agreement without speaking as Dave looked at them in turn.

"You've got a deal, Mr. Watters," Dave said.

They shook hands again, and without anything but a nod to each of them, Watters walked away.

"It looks like you're in business, Dave," Comer said.

"That's a lot of starting money for around here," Roger said. "I was afraid for a minute you were going to turn him down."

"Uh uh," Dave said. "People don't offer me money that often."

That's not quite true, he thought. That was a slight exaggeration. It was the first time he had ever been offered starting money.

When he thought about this, it was a little frightening. Starting money was paid by race promoters anxious to provide their customers with crowd pleasers. There were, viewed somewhat cynically, only two kinds of crowd pleasers, the fools and the daredevils, who could almost be counted upon to have at least one spectacular crash during a race program, and the winners. Crowds, whose admission tickets entirely supported the sport at the smaller tracks, would pay to see a winner.

He had done nothing today that would suggest he was a

daredevil. He hadn't scratched the paint. He'd won two races and placed ninth of eleven in the major race. He didn't think that Watters was any more a fool than Uncle Comer. That meant that Watters felt he was going to be a winner. Charley had said that he was good, and Roger Chedister had echoed that.

He felt confident and yet not at all confident. He'd wanted this very badly, but now that it was apparently happening, it was frightening. There was a good chance that he had been lucky, that circumstances had developed to make him look a great deal better than he really was. There was a good chance that when the day of reckoning came, a great deal more than his pride would be damaged.

He found that Roger was looking at him oddly.

"You all right, Dave?"

"Sure," Dave said. "I'm a little hungry, I guess."

He wondered then why a man had to be ashamed of being afraid, why it was necessary to conceal from everyone the fact that you had considered all the facts and were scared. But he was doing it, just as everybody else did it.

"I'll buy," he said. "Providing your tastes don't go any higher than the dollar-fifty special."

"I got a better idea than that," Uncle Comer said.

"Oh?"

"Roger, Charley and I were talking," Comer said, "while you were out there chasing your own tail."

"Is that so?" Dave said, and he smiled because he felt that he was expected to smile.

"That's so," Comer said. "And we decided that if you

were willing to part with some of the stock of Motor Enterprises, Inc., in other words, if you were willing to take in a couple of partners, you just might find a couple of people right around here you could do business with."

"I wonder who?" Dave said.

"We were thinking that we could go fifty-fifty before expenses," Comer said, and he still sounded as if he were making the proposition as a joke, even though it was obvious to all of them that he wasn't joking at all.

"Can't we talk about it while we eat?" Dave asked. He was afraid that he wasn't thinking as clearly as he should be thinking.

"We can talk on the way, I suppose," Comer said. "Is there any real reason you have to load the car on the trailer now? Can't we go eat and then come back when the crowd is gone and get it?"

"Why not?" Dave said.

They went to a restaurant on U.S. Highway 90 which had tables outside under an awning, and where the customers seemed to understand why so many of the patrons were so dirty and grease stained.

Dave was still thirsty, so thirsty that he drank first one large glass of milk and then a second. He remembered that he hadn't eaten before the races. He wondered whether this had been because he was so excited about racing that he'd forgotten or so frightened that he hadn't had any appetite.

Whatever the reason, he was now starved.

As he ate all of a steak guaranteed to weigh at least twenty-four ounces when served, with a large baked potato and a huge bowl of salad, Uncle Comer explained his proposition. There was no nonsense about it.

What Comer proposed wasn't much different than the original organization of Motor Enterprises. There would be a manager, a mechanic, and a driver. The whole purpose was to make money. If fun could be had as a by-product, well then, fine, but the avowed purpose was to make money.

The roles were different. Dave before had been mechanic, manager, and supplier of equipment. Now he was the driver. Roger would now be the manager, and Dave understood that Roger would be a different kind of a manager than he himself had been.

Roger expected to give the orders. He might give them politely, and he might even seek advice and ideas, but he would give orders not make suggestions.

Comer would put up the cash for entry fees and the like, and would also pay for parts and facilities to maintain the cars. No longer would the Motor Enterprises Special be rebuilt with hand tools out of a tool box.

Comer spoke slowly, carefully, and almost alone. There were nods from Roger Chedister and Charley, but they seldom said more than one word, and that was only "Sure," or "Right."

Basically, the proposition made to him was simple. In exchange for his interest in the wrecked Motor Enterprises Special, the pizza wagon, the trailer, and all the spare parts, plus his services as driver, they would relieve him of all financial responsibility. They would, in other words, pay all the bills, and, moreover, give him fifty percent of all the money they took in.

They were gambling, in other words, that their cars, and his ability to dri e would make enough money in prizes and starting money to give them all a profit. Dave had a reaction he was a little ashamed of. At least, he thought, as he nodded his agreement on a minor point Comer had made, no one's mother is going to wreck this partnership by demanding her money back.

That was sort of a childish reaction, he thought. He also felt sure that he had paid close attention, and that the proposition offered was more than fair. Furthermore, he would have taken any proposition offered by Comer, expecting it to be fair and honest and just, because Comer was that sort of man.

"What do you say, Dave?" Comer asked.

"How are you, partner?" Dave replied.

"Do you want it in writing?" Comer asked.

"No, sir. That's not necessary."

"We'll put it in writing," Roger Chedister said, not argumentatively, but as a statement of fact. "I don't think any contract is worth more than the character of the people that sign it, but having it around will help remind us what the original agreement was."

"He's right," Comer said.

"Not only am I right, but I'm managing this menagerie," Chedister said.

They chuckled because they were expected to, but they all knew that Chedister wasn't joking at all.

"I'll go down to the judge's office tomorrow," Comer said.

"I'd appreciate it," Roger said. "And I'd like the keys to the garage, if Charley doesn't have them."

Comer took a thick ring of keys from his pockets and went through them slowly until he found what he was looking for. He separated two keys from the others and handed them over to Chedister.

"I'll get Charley a set made tomorrow," he said. "Are you planning to go down there first thing in the morning?"

Comer had very carefully given the keys to Chedister before asking him what he was going to do with them. He had very carefully made it clear that Chedister had an unquestioned right to the keys.

Dave was considering this when Chedister answered, "I'm going down there with Charley tonight. I want to take a quick look at the big car."

"You want me to go with you?" Dave asked.

"I don't think so, Dave. Thanks just the same," Chedister said. "I'll see you down there about eight-thirty, if that's all right?"

"Sure," Dave said. He had avoided just in time, saying "Yes, sir."

"Why don't you get that inch of crud scraped off you and go look up whatsername, the blonde?" Roger suggested.

"Her name is Anne," Dave said.

"I've got an idea that he would like me to remember that in the future," Roger said, and he laughed, and Comer and Charley laughed with him. This made it impossible for

Dave to become angry, although he was. He didn't mind being told when to race or even how, but it was obviously going to be necessary to let Roger know that his manager's duties stopped at the race track.

"Come on," Comer said as Dave drained his coffee cup, "we'll take you home and see if we can't sneak you through the kitchen door so that Marge won't see you."

Dave was reminded that Comer was an automobile dealer when Comer forced him to wait until he had spread a protective cloth over the upholstery of the car before he would permit Dave to sit on it.

They did not succeed in fooling either Aunt Marge or Aunt Leslie. The women were waiting in the kitchen. "Where have you been?"

"We stopped to get something to eat," Comer said.

"You forgot there's a refrigerator full of food here?" Marge asked sarcastically.

"I didn't think you'd want to make a steak dinner at half-past ten at night, to tell the truth," Comer said.

"You let that boy eat a full dinner at this time of night? What's the matter with you?" Marge challenged.

"You can't win, Dave," Comer said, unruffled.

"Are you still hungry?" Marge asked.

"No, ma'am," Dave said.

"Leslie made a chocolate cake," Marge said.

"Give him a piece," Aunt Leslie ordered. "He'll eat it."

And he did. He ate while Comer related all the details of the racing. The facts were all there, Dave heard, but Comer had rather skillfully omitted the wrecks. He didn't mention the partnership, but did announce that Dave was offered, and had accepted, $250 starting money from the track in Bainbridge, Georgia.

Aunt Marge had no comment to make. And then Aunt Leslie closed the discussion, saying "He's dirty, he's tired, and I suppose he'll be down messing with those dirty cars first thing in the morning. You go up and take a shower and go to bed, Dave."

"Yes, ma'am," he said.

He soaked in the bathtub a long time to relax his muscles, and when he was completely bathed, he showered. He stood under the pounding water for a long time because he knew that he simply would not be able to fall asleep. Too much had happened. Forming the partnership was enough in itself. One race would have kept him up all night, and he had raced three times. Winning once would have kept him up all night, and he had won twice.

He resigned himself to tossing and turning all night. He lay down on the bed, and put his hands under his face and curled up. He took one deep breath and was dead to the world.

_____ Nine

W HAT HE THOUGHT of first
when he woke in the morning had
nothing whatever to do with quick-change rear ends, hemi-
spherical pistons, Holley carburetors or compression ratios.
After he dressed, but before he went to the kitchen, he went
to the telephone. "Good morning, Mrs. Wagner, this is Dave
Wade. Could I speak to Anne, please?"

She sounded sleepy when she came to the phone, and he
caught himself before he got carried away. The reason she
was sleepy was that she had been up late, and the reason she
had been up late is because she had been out with Rufus,
and the reason . . .

"Hello, Dave," she said. "Is anything the matter?"

"I'm sorry to get you up," he said.

"I've been up," she said.

"I called about tonight," he said.

"What about tonight?"

"I got the impression," he said, "that you said you would

be willing to ride in the old station wagon."

"I did."

"Can I pick you up about seven-thirty?" he asked.

"All right," she said.

"Well, O.K., I'll see you then."

"O.K.," Anne said. There was a pause, during which neither of them could think of anything to say, and then Anne hung up first.

When he put the telephone back into its cradle, he held his hand on it a moment. He wondered why he wanted to date a girl he couldn't talk to, and with whom he argued like an English bulldog and a belligerent Cheshire cat. He smiled at himself when he thought of the answer . . . because I have a weakness for blue-eyed blondes.

Comer was already gone when Dave sat down for breakfast.

"What time does he open up?" Dave asked, in surprise, because it wasn't quite eight o'clock, and it was only a ten-minute drive from the house to the garage and showroom.

"Six," Aunt Marge said. "This is the country, Dave. We sell tractors and trucks. When a farmer's truck won't start or his tractor's got a leak in the hydraulic system, he wants it fixed then, so he can do a day's work, not wait around until say nine o'clock, for the mechanics to come to work."

"I should have thought of that," Dave said, embarrassed.

"There's no shame in sleeping late after a good night's work," Aunt Marge said, "and apparently you did a good night's work last night."

"Yes, ma'am."

"We talked about it after you went to bed," Aunt Marge said. "I won't say I'm convinced that you're right, but I'll admit I'm awful proud of it."

"Thank you."

"But I'm a little disappointed, too," she said.

"Something I did?"

"Something it looks like you're not going to do," she said, and then, before he had to ask for an explanation, she went on. "I sort of hoped that you'd be on a vacation down here. But you came down here and went right to work."

"Sort of a vacation for me," Dave said. "I like it."

"Comer said that you wouldn't have to do much of the mechanic work, now that Charley's working with you. And he's agreed that this should be more of a vacation for you than working."

Dave looked at her. She was obviously ill at ease.

"I've got a suspicion," he said, finally, "that you haven't quite finished saying what you had planned to say."

"No," she admitted.

"If you make me wait any more," Dave said, knowing that it couldn't be anything really serious and sorry that she was so worried about his reaction, "I'll start to blush and giggle."

She laughed then, a great deal louder than the poor joke justified, convincing him that he was right. Now he grew mock stern, raised his right hand in a fist with the index finger extended.

"Out with it!" he said, gesturing like the villain in a silent movie.

"It's nothing that bad," she said. "It's just that I thought you should be around with young people your own age."

"I agree," he said. "Is that all? Or did you have something?"

"There's a group going down to the beach this afternoon," she said. "And I thought you would like to go . . ."

"No," he protested. "I've got to work on the car."

She ignored this.

"And I arranged for you to go. With a girl."

"Oh, Boy!" he said.

"And now I realize that I made a mistake, and I'm sorry," she said.

"I'll go," he said. "You're right."

"You're being nice," she said.

"No, I mean it," he said. "I'd like to go down on the beach this afternoon."

"Now you shush," Aunt Marge said. "It won't happen again, and I can simply call Helen Wagner and tell her that I didn't know you had to work."

"Mrs. Wagner?" Dave interrupted.

"Yes. You'd met Anne, and I thought . . ."

"If you go near that telephone, you'll have to wrestle me," Dave said.

She looked at him for a moment and saw that his smile had changed from one of polite determination to one of genuine pleasure.

"I gather you like the idea now that Anne is a part of it?"

"I just called her up and asked her to go out tonight,"

Dave said. "Just now, just before I came down for breakfast."

"Really?"

"Really."

"Well," Aunt Marge said, and she turned and filled his milk glass for the third time, and then looked at the empty half-gallon bottle as if she was confused. "I'd have sworn that this was full when I took it from the refrigerator," she said.

"What time am I supposed to be there?" he asked.

"Twelve thirty. Comer said he'd arrange for you to get a car down at the showroom. You could hardly drive her to Panama City in the pizza wagon."

He was late to pick up Anne, of course. When he got to the garage, Roger and Charley were already there and already at work, stripping the Motor Enterprises Special to the chassis. There was work to do, and he was qualified to do it, and the three of them worked almost in silence for more than two hours, unbolting components, setting them away from the chassis in several unnamed but quite distinct piles: Salvageable as is; Repairable; Not Repairable; Usable; Usable, but let's think about using something better.

It was evident that Roger had quickly earned Charley's complete confidence, and equally evident that Roger was going to take nothing for granted. The second spare engine (despite Dave's success at Alafla with the first spare engine in the old Ford) would not be used in the Special.

Roger made this announcement off-the-cuff. Charley was using the transmission cradle, a heavy steel-wheeled device used to move heavy parts by hand, to move the engine installed in the wrecked Special out of the way.

"While you're at it, Charley, you might as well move that other engine for the old car out of the way. We won't be needing that for a while, unless Dave bends it up some."

Charley nodded his agreement.

"You're planning to use that engine in the old Ford?" Dave asked, making sure that his voice was level and as disinterested as he could make it.

"I'd rather, Dave," Roger said. "We've got too much going on the big car to take any chances."

"How long are we going to run the old Ford?"

"Oh, until it earns its keep or begins to cost us money. Or you drive it into the grandstands. I don't think we could get much for it, selling it. And we've already got an investment in parts and engines."

Dave nodded. He didn't like the feeling, but it was there. It, whatever it was, had been taken away from him. He was no longer lord and master of all that he surveyed. He had been put in a niche and assigned duties, and while it was obvious that the team wasn't much use without him, it was just as obvious that he was no longer the whole show, and very obvious that he was not the team's captain.

He thought about this, and then he told himself that he should grow up, that he knew better. He did pretty well at this. When he found himself stripping the tires and tubes from all the wheels, so that the tires could get a thorough examination and the wheels could be tested for trueness and for internal flaws with a magnafluxing machine, he told himself that he really hadn't been demoted all the way back to where he had begun in the industry, changing tires at the Lewis Super Service Station. He was just carrying his share of the load.

He could add to this. He was testing wheels and tires, not just changing flats; and the wheels and tires he was testing were the ones he would be racing on.

"Where are we going to get those tested, Charley?" Roger asked.

"Tires we can handle," Charley said. "But the nearest magnaflux machine is in Dothan."

"Have you got time to run them up there?" Roger asked Dave, looking at him. Dave had just about been prepared to feel sorry for himself. He had quickly decided that it didn't take any mystical ability to foretell the future to guess who was going to drive back and forth to Dothan.

Now, when Roger asked him (and asked him, not told him) to go he felt ashamed of himself again. He was behaving like a petulant child. He wanted to take his ball and go home because the game wasn't going his way.

"Sure," he said. "Plenty of time."

"I hate to ask you," Roger said, and Dave knew that this wasn't something Roger was saying to please him, but that he meant it, "but it looks like we'll lose a couple of days, otherwise."

"No problem at all."

Roger winked at him. "Give my regards to whatsername," he said. "And don't get eaten by a shark."

Dave rolled the wheels to the pizza wagon and lifted

them in, one by one. He had just finished fastening them with nylon straps he'd bought at an Army-Navy surplus store when Charley stuck his head through the folding door.

"Comer says he's left a car for you at the showroom, and that you should go there, and he'll get the truck back here."

"Thanks."

The pizza truck admittedly wasn't the fastest thing on the highways, but, as Dave rolled noisily on toward Dothan, just across the Alabama border, it seemed to be crawling. And the sweep second hand on the watch seemed to have picked up speed.

He was going to be late for his first date with Anne. There was no question about that, and, when he thought about it, it seemed to be entirely expected.

Then he got lost in Dothan finding the machine shop equipped with the magnafluxing machine. When he finally got there, rock salt was liberally dumped into his bleeding ego by the grease-covered, young man left in charge, who took one look at the Luigi's Neapolitan pizza advertisement and volunteered the information that the shop "didn't fool around none fixing old trucks."

"I've got some wheels here for magnafluxing," Dave said.

"For that?"

"For Roger Chedister," Dave said, and it actually hurt him to keep smiling.

"Oh. Why didn't you say so? How long you been working for Roger?"

"Since last night," Dave said, telling himself that was almost true. "He said he'd give me a chance."

"Good luck," the young man said.

"Where do you want the wheels?" Dave said, as he opened the rear door of the pizza wagon.

"Put them anywhere over there against the wall," the young man said, gesturing with his hand, not even looking at Dave.

Dave decided he would rather lie on the track in front of the whole pack just before the flag went down than ask this fellow for help. And, because he was working as quickly as he could and was just about as angry as he could get, he managed to drop two wheels. One fell on his left foot, on the toes, and the second took a good half-inch of skin from the left index finger.

Back on the four-lane highway out of Dothan, he saw that the pizza wagon was very nearly out of gas. This was the crowning blow. He got back to Marianna, sweaty, dirty, scarred, and angry five minutes late for his date with Anne.

"This is Dave Wade, Mrs. Wagner," he said, over the parts-room telephone in the garage. "Would you please tell Anne . . ."

"She's on the extension, Dave," Anne's mother said. "Aren't you, Dear?"

"Hi," she said.

"I'm sorry, but I was delayed and I'm going to be a little late," Dave said.

"I know," she said.

"I beg your pardon?"

"Roger called and said you had to go to Dothan and would be late."

"Oh."

"So I knew."

"I'll be there in forty-five minutes."

"Don't rush," she said. "The others have gone already."

"I'll be there as soon as I can," he said, and hung up.

Good old Roger handled every little detail, apparently. What was the matter? Why the resentment? He should be grateful.

He went to the shop foreman, because that seemed to be the best place to find out what car Comer had arranged for him to use, and where he could find it. On the way, he saw, and simply couldn't pass because he thought it was like a work of art, a brand-new powder-blue New Yorker convertible with white leather upholstery. The top was down, and it was freshly polished, glistening, and obviously just about to be delivered to some lucky character.

Just beautiful, he decided. And another corner of his mind added that it was a soundly engineered car too, with many of the characteristics of the Chrysler 300 when that had been a bona fide, high performance machine.

"What do you think, Dave?" the shop foreman asked, coming over to him.

"I think it must be nice to be rich," Dave said. "Money might not buy happiness, but I don't think I could really be too miserable in that."

The shop foreman laughed.

"I guess I'd better get you a drop cloth," he said. "You're pretty greasy."

"Yes, sir. And you'd better show me what I'm to drive,

too, please."

"You're looking at it."

"You're kidding."

"Not at all."

"I don't want to drive that," Dave said automatically, and what he meant was that he was afraid or embarrassed to drive it, that he didn't want to impose on Comer's generosity. For a moment the shop foreman misunderstood him.

"Then they didn't give you your fair share of sense," he said. When understanding came, he added, "Dave, we always put one of those in the showroom. First car we generally get is the fancy convertible. Comer says it gets people inside to look. They don't buy the convertible. But they look at it, and then they buy something else. Convertible just sits there. We generally have to discount it pretty heavily at the end of the model year just to sell it. And I don't have to tell you that just sitting doesn't do a car a bit of good."

That was true, Dave knew that. Unless the parts of a machine designed to move were moved, too much stress from weight began to tear them down. Shock absorbers lost their strength; tires, especially nylon tires, acquired a permanent set, or flat spot, where they touched the ground; and, finally, oil dripped off higher parts of the engine so that it was bone-dry when started again. A sitting car deteriorated.

Well, it was too late to argue about it, and it seemed, when he thought about it, to be just another indication that he could, with no effort at all, behave as if he were six years old.

He opened the door gingerly, and then reconsidered. He let it close by itself, and went to a drum of solvent and dipped his hands in. By the time he'd dried them and saw that if they weren't exactly lily-white, they would not leave a mark on whatever he touched, the shop foreman had draped a drop cloth over the driver's seat.

Dave expected a difference between the pizza wagon and this car, but he was not prepared for the degree of difference. This was the model equipped with what Detroit called all the pizazz. Everything was automatic. The seat of the pizza wagon was artificial leather, over lumpy cotton padding, over steel springs. This seat was soft, genuine leather, over foam rubber, over soft springs, and electric motors moved it up and down and even tilted it. The suspension and steering of the pizza wagon precisely amplified every crack in the concrete, pebble, and rut over which the wagon drove. The steering here was hydraulically assisted, and the suspension, Dave decided, was so good that it would probably not transmit the shock of running over a curb.

And the transmission. Automatic, and so smooth that Dave had to concentrate to detect the automatic change of gear ratio.

Only an idiot, he decided, as he got near the house, would complain about being allowed to drive a car like this.

It took him fifteen minutes to shower, dress, pick up his bathing suit and get back in the car, and another ten minutes to get to Anne's house. She was waiting for him on the porch, and he appreciated this. He had been late for dates before, but late, on time, or early, he had never gone out with a girl who had not required that he wait for her.

She saw him coming and even came off the porch to meet him.

"Hi," she said, pulling open the door and getting in. Dave had nothing whatever against opening the door for the fair sex, and actually rather enjoyed it when it seemed to fit. But this, he decided, would have been one of those almost ludicrous encounters. He would have had to stop the car, put on the parking brake, shut off the engine, unfasten the seat belt, run around the front of the car, hold the door for her, and then start from scratch, buckling the seat belt, starting the engine, and releasing the brake before finally moving again.

"I'm sorry I'm late," he said as he moved off.

Anne nodded her head, accepting the apology and dismissing it. "What's magnaflux mean?" she asked.

"I don't really know," he admitted, after he thought for a moment. "It's an X ray process of some kind. What it does is detect internal flaws in metal obejcts."

"Oh," she said. She looked up from fastening her belt. "Go down to the end of the block and turn left. You'll come to an old hotel. Turn right, and keep going."

"How far is it?"

"Fifty miles," she said. "But it's all back-country roads, and you can make pretty good time." She paused, and then asked, "Are you a dangerous driver?"

"I don't think so," he said, a little sharply.

"I mean," she said, "I don't like to go fast."

"What you probably mean," Dave said, aware that he

was unable to avoid an argument by simply keeping his mouth shut, "is that you don't like to go too fast for conditions."

He waited for her response to this, and was surprised when all she said was, "I suppose that's right, when I think about it." And then she smiled at him, as if she had inspected him and found him satisfactory.

The drive down to Panama City was pleasant. There were enough miles on the car (apparently put there by salesmen giving demonstration rides) so that Dave could drive it at (and just above) the speed limit without worrying about breaking the car in.

He knew that the speedometer indicated a higher speed than the car was actually going. In a cynical mood, he often wondered if the manufacturers hadn't intended it to be that way. Speed was certainly a selling point, and if customers got the impression they were going faster than they really were, they were likely to be pleased.

Dave had long before come to the conclusion that automobile manufacturers gave the customer what he thought he wanted not what was good for him. At about the same time, he had decided that manufacturers designed parts of their cars to wear out in a couple of years so the owner would be tempted to buy a new one. Proof of this, he thought, was the door. At one time, a metal molding which was nearly impossible to wear out had been at the top of the door, near the glass, where the arm of the driver rested and where the driver and passenger were likely to push and pull to open and close the door. The metal strip had just about vanished, and, now, upholstery went all the way to the glass. Upholstery, of course, could be counted upon to fray and discolor and wear out in a couple of years.

These were unpleasant and cynical thoughts, thoughts having no place in the mind of a young man out with a pretty, blonde girl in a shining convertible, and on his way to the beach on a sunny summer day. He put them out of his mind and cheered himself with the thought that today, at least, he would not have to put up with Rufus. Today, he would have Anne all to himself. The fact that they were meeting some twenty-odd others didn't seem at all important, just so long as Rufus would not be around.

They went through Panama City and over the sweeping bridge to Panama City Beach, and, finally, Anne pointed, "There they are," she said, and he braked. He saw that there was a place to park right beside Rufus' Thunderbird. Rufus was leaning on it drinking a coke, and his face bore a look of patient resignation. It was obvious he had been waiting for them.

Ten

EVERYONE was polite and friendly, and just about everyone smiled at him, but Dave felt that he was an outsider, and worse, that he was being tolerated. He felt, he told himself, as he stood up, impulsively ran toward the Gulf of Mexico, and took a running dive into the water, very much as an ugly girl for whom a blind date had been arranged must feel.

Everyone tries to be nice, and the nicer everyone is, the more the ugly duckling feels like an unwanted object of sympathy. He wanted Anne's interest, not her sympathy. She was obviously being nice to him because her mother and Aunt Marge were long-time friends.

And Rufus, good old Rufus, was being so considerate and charming. Dave realized, as he surfaced and then ducked under an incoming wave, that he was being 'damned with faint praise.' One of the subjects in political science had been propaganda, and the phrase and the technique had stuck in Dave's mind, together with some other useless information.

He wondered if Rufus had taken the same sort of course wherever he went to school or whether it had come naturally to him. Dave was aware that his sole claim to fame was the fact that he had done rather well at the Alafla Track. Rufus had very neatly cut him in half. "Even with that car, Dave—and let me tell you, we don't see that kind of power in a quarter-mile car very much around here—I think you should be proud of the way you placed."

The implication was clear that the reason Dave had placed was because he had a larger, more powerful engine. Rufus made it very plain that this was, somehow, an unfair advantage. Dave knew that he would prove Rufus' point if he disputed what he said. Rufus was clever.

All's fair in love and war.

Is that what it was? Was he angry with Rufus simply because he was jealous? Or could he trust the instinct that told him that Rufus was simply a louse?

He swam for fifteen minutes, not resting, taking long, powerful strokes, forcing himself not to think about going back to the beach and to concentrate on moving through the water. When he finally rolled over on his back, floated, and found the beach by turning his head, he felt a great deal better. It was too beautiful a day, really, to be angry about anything. He floated for a couple of minutes, and then swam toward shore until he could drop his feet and touch bottom. Then he waded back to the beach through the surf.

Anne was on her feet, shaking the sand from the beach

towel (a huge representation of the Confederate Flag) on which she had been lying. She had a terry cloth jacket over her bathing suit, a straw hat on her head, and sandals on her feet. It was obvious that she was going somewhere.

"Where've you been?" she said. "Rufus said he told you we were going up the beach for giantburgers."

Rufus hadn't said a thing about going anywhere. But Dave decided that it wouldn't be right to call him a liar; there was a chance that it was simply a misunderstanding.

"Where is Rufus?" he asked, taking the towel from her, folding it, trying to smile.

"Waiting for us by the cars," she said.

"I'm sorry I'm holding things up," Dave said.

"No harm. We've been late all day, why break the pattern?"

It could have been sarcastic, but her smile softened it, and he decided that she was just, again, being nice.

"Come on," he said. "We'll try to be on time from now on."

Rufus and another man and a girl were standing by his Thunderbird.

"I told you we'd meet you," Anne said sharply to him. "You could have gone ahead."

"Well, there's two reasons we didn't," Rufus said, and he smiled. "The first is that we didn't want you to get left, in case ol' Dave here drowned or got himself eaten by a shark during the long distance swim of his, and the second is that when we got here, we saw that some unpleasant individual spilled his malted milk all over Dave's upholstery, and that there'd be no place for you to sit."

Dave looked into the car. Someone indeed had spilled a malted milk, a chocolate malted milk, on the door and front seat of the car.

"Oh, isn't that a shame!" Anne said.

"You just can't tell what some people will do," Rufus said.

Dave thought, I'll give even money that you won't lose much sleep over this tonight.

"We figured we'd better wait here and see if we could help clean it up for you," Rufus said, the picture of concerned friendship.

"I'll tell you what, Rufus," Dave said. "Why don't you take Anne with you, and I'll catch up to you? There's no sense everybody standing around in the sun. There's a gas station over there, and I'll get it cleaned up there."

"I'll stay, Dave," Anne said. "I can help."

"Tell you what I'll do, Dave," Rufus said, the good, trusted friend eager to do his best. "I'll walk over there with you, and see that you'll be all right."

Dave forced down another wave of anger. What Rufus had suggested was that Dave wasn't bright enough to cross the street by himself and ask for water and rags and whatever else would be needed to clean the car's upholstery. Not trusting himself to speak, he nodded and got in the car and drove across the highway to the gas station. Rufus followed on foot. "You sure you don't need any help?" he asked.

"Sure. Thanks just the same," Dave said.

"Well, then, I guess you're right. There's no sense in having Anne wait in the hot sun. We'll meet you at The Surf. Do you know where it is?"

"No."

"Just go down the beach highway. It's on the right, and you can't miss it," Rufus said. "We'll wait for you there."

"Fine," Dave said. "You go ahead."

He stood there and waited until the Thunderbird had gone up the highway and then returned Anne's wave. He told himself that he had done the right thing. He had kept his temper and not sworn, although the mess in the car was a strong temptation, and he had seen to it that Anne had not been inconvenienced. When they were out of sight, he went into the station office.

"I've got some malted milk on my upholstery," he said. "Can I get something to take it off?"

"Sure," the proprietor said, but he cocked his head and looked at Dave strangely.

"Something wrong?"

"Who's the big guy in the Thunderbird?" the proprietor asked. "He pledging you for a fraternity or something?"

"No. Why?"

"Well, then, maybe you could tell me why you're cleaning up what he spilled."

"He spilled it? You're sure."

"I watched him. Thought for a minute the way he was pouring it in there that the seat was on fire or something."

"Well, I'll tell you," Dave said. "The truth of the matter is, when you get right down to it, that I'm a little backward. Up North, where I come from, they'd say I was pretty stupid."

"I got some stuff here," the proprietor said, "costs a dollar ninety-eight. Guaranteed to remove, among other things, milk stains without a trace."

"Let's see if it works," Dave said.

It took almost an hour to clean the upholstery, and the label on the can of upholstery cleaner wasn't exactly accurate. There was a spot on the seat, and another on the door upholstery where the milk, syrup, and ice-cream mixture had been. It wouldn't have mattered much, Dave knew, had this car already been sold, but to sell the car, the otherwise insignificant spot would force a reduction in price way out of proportion to the real damage.

He spent a full forty-five minutes looking for The Surf, and when he found it, there was no red Thunderbird, no Anne, and right now, most important, no Rufus. When he had time to think about it, later, he could not remember ever being quite so furious about anything.

Then, by accident, he saw the taillights of a Thunderbird parked behind another beach-side hamburger stand. He pulled off to the right, waited five minutes until the flow of traffic permitted him to cross the street, and then pulled into the drive-in parking lot.

He thought that the wait had been valuable. He was in no mood to confront Rufus with Anne present. He peered through the window, saw the four of them at a table, and then asked a waitress, an unpleasant looking young woman, to ask Rufus to come outside for a moment.

"Why don't you tell him yourself?"

Dave reached in his pocket and handed over a dollar bill.

"Please?" he asked.

"Why not?"

He leaned on the tile wall of the drive-in, forgetting that it had been exposed to the sun's heat all day. It was hot enough to burn him and it did. He jumped away.

"Well, look who's here," Rufus said, smiling broadly. "My favorite little Yankee. I thought we'd seen the last of you, for today."

"I figure you owe me a dollar ninety-eight, Rufus," Dave said.

"What for?"

"For cleaning stuff for the upholstery."

"You know what I owe you, little Yankee? I owe you my profound thanks for bringing my girl down here. And that's all. Now why don't you get back in Uncle Comer's car and just go away, huh? Like a good guy? Before I have to pound you into the ground like a tent stake?"

Dave hit him as hard as he could, a right cross aimed at his jaw. Rufus pulled his chin back, so that he was struck only a glancing blow, and then, quickly, skillfully, hit Dave twice, a left to the face, and then a right to the solar plexus, and Dave found himself sitting down hard on the pebbles in the drive. He got to his feet and started for Rufus again. Suddenly, he felt himself stopped, clamped firmly in strong arms.

"Let me go," he tried to say, and was surprised that it came out a shout. "I'll kill him."

"You just calm down, Boy," the voice said, and Dave

jerked his head around angrily to see not only who was insulting him, but adding insult to that injury by calling him Boy and offering advice. He looked right into the eyes of a large, florid-faced and angry-looking officer of the law. Dave stopped struggling. After a moment's wait, the bearlike grip relaxed, but a firm, and large hand, remained on each arm.

"What's this all about?" the policeman asked.

"I just told him to stay away from my girl," Rufus said, "and I guess he got a little mad."

"Is that so?" the policeman asked of Dave.

"She's not his girl," Dave said.

"See? " Rufus asked, reasonably.

"The girl in there?"

"Yes, sir," Rufus replied, the picture of the polite, well-bred, non-brawling young man.

"Well, I'll believe you," the policeman said. "You take her out that way," he nodded with his head in one direction, "and I'll take this young fella this way," he nodded with his head in the opposite direction. "And that will remove the source of friction."

"Yes, sir," Rufus said, grateful, humble. "I'm sorry this happened, sir."

"It's happened before, and it'll happen again," the policeman said. "Now, go on, get her out of here."

Dave allowed himself to be taken around the side of the building. The policeman didn't say a word for a full three minutes, and then, finally, he said. "You stay here, hear?"

"Yes, sir," Dave said.

The policeman looked into the drive-in, and then walked behind Dave and looked in the rear parking lot. Dave was uncomfortably aware that a crowd of people had gathered and were looking at him with shameless fascination.

"Well, they seem to be gone," the policeman said. "You got any identification, Son?"

"Yes, sir," Dave said and produced his driver's license.

"You're a long way from home?" the policeman said, and he made it a question.

"Yes, sir."

"How'd you get here? Today, I mean?"

"I drove."

"You got your car here?"

"Yes, sir."

"Where is it?"

"The blue one."

"That fancy convertible?"

"Yes, sir. It belongs to my uncle."

"I see," the policeman said. He went and looked over the car.

"It belongs to your uncle, you say?"

"Yes, sir."

"You never get away with lying to the police, son," the policeman said. "That's just a rule of life. Now where did you get that car?"

"From my uncle."

"You got the registration for it?"

Dave's stomach contracted.

"No, sir."

"You wait here," the policeman said. He walked to the Chrysler and pulled the keys from the lock. When he came back, he took Dave's arm and led him to a black, four-door Chevrolet. He opened the door for him, motioned him inside and slammed the door. There were no handles on the inside of the door, and there was a closely knit, wire mesh between the front and the back seats.

The policeman blinked his red light and let the siren growl so that he could get into the steady line of traffic, and then, as they drove along the beach highway, with people looking with fascination into the back seat, he picked up the radio microphone.

"This is Twenty-seven," he said.

"Go ahead, Twenty-seven."

"I got what may be a hot car here. Deserves looking into, anyway. Check with the Motor Vehicle Bureau and see who owns dealer's license plate V-2333."

"Kerr Motors, in Marianna," Dave said from the back seat.

"And while you're at it, have the Marianna police check with Kerr Motors and see if they're missing a new blue Chrysler convertible."

The policeman turned his head halfway around.

"Take us ten, fifteen minutes to get to the station, Son," he said gently, even kindly. "You just keep your mouth shut until we get there, and see if you don't decide when you think about it that the best thing you can do is just tell the truth and get the whole thing over with."

In two hours, Dave was free. He had pleaded guilty to

driving a motor vehicle on the public highways of the State of Florida without having upon his person the documentation required by law, and had paid a fine of $10, plus $2.50 costs.

Comer knew not only the policeman who had arrested Dave, but the desk sergeant, the chief of detectives and the chief of police. During their polite, old friends conversation, Dave heard, and it hurt to hear, the remark that it was the first time "old Comer'd ever been down to the jailhouse."

The highway patrol had found him on the farm, and driven him to Panama City. A Panama City police car drove Comer and Dave back to the drive-in, where the convertible sat glistening in the sun.

"Comer, I'm sorry we had to jail him," the chief of detectives said. "But he didn't have the registration, and he sure didn't sound like he was from Marianna, Florida."

"My fault about the registration," Comer said. "It'll teach us both a lesson. I'm grateful to you. What if it had been stolen? And the fella who stole it had a good southern accent?"

"I'm sorry I caused all the trouble," Dave said, and it sounded even to him as if he were muttering from the bottom of a well.

"You caused yourself all the trouble, Son," the chief of detectives said. Then he laughed. "Didn't Comer ever tell you that fighting's not very bright to begin with, and hitting somebody with four inches and fifty pounds on you borders on the stupid?"

"I guess he didn't figure he had to," Dave said.

"You drive, Dave," Comer said. "I'm tired."

They drove in silence until they were out of town, and on the lonely road leading home to Marianna.

"I'm sorry, Comer," Dave said.

"You gave us quite a scare," Comer admitted. "But I don't think the world will stop turning. You want to tell me all about it?"

"Yes, sir. I figure I owe you that," Dave said. And when he turned to look at Comer, he saw the stained door panel. "And for that too. I'll replace that."

"What happened to it?" Comer asked, but before Dave could reply, he said, "Start at the beginning."

Dave told everything, even making the humiliating confession that he had wound up sitting down on the gravel with the breath knocked out of him after he'd swung at Rufus.

"That boy is mean," Comer said. "I've always thought so. His father was shiftless, and he's shiftless."

"Where does he get his money?"

"Their granddaddy owned some useless land. The Air Force wanted it for a range for Elgin Air Force Base. For serial gunnery. Their granddaddy had enough sense not to sell it. He rents it. Doesn't do a thing to earn his keep except cash the government's check."

"Oh."

Comer shrugged and lapsed into silence.

"Comer, I'm really sorry that it's turned out this way. I'm sorry as I can be. I'll get out of town as quietly as I can."

"You can't do that, Dave," Comer said.

"I embarrassed you. I embarrassed Aunt Marge. And I made a three-star fool of myself."

"Well, let's say you lost a fight," Comer said. "But you can't go, Dave."

"Why not?"

"Well, for one thing, it would be turn_ng tail to the likes of Rufus. And for another, I invested about five thousand dollars in you this afternoon."

"Sir?"

"Well, Roger and I decided that trying to fix that wrecked car would be sort of like throwing good money after bad, so we junked it. And I telephoned to the assembly plant and had them send us a stripped Fury. Should be here tomorrow."

"Comer, do you know how much money it costs to prepare a Grand National car?"

"We figure, not counting the use of the equipment, that it'll be right about twenty-two, twenty-three thousand. Tires and spares and so on included."

"And you're going to trust me with that?"

"Why not? Roger says you're the best natural driver he's ever seen. And we just proved that you've got what they call the 'scrappy spirit.' "

"What about Aunt Marge? What am I going to say to her?"

"The truth. You got locked up because I didn't give you the registration to that car. She'll blame me for that."

"What am I going to say to Anne?" Dave heard himself

ask.

"That's one problem, Dave," Comer said, chuckling, "that you're just going to have to answer yourself."

For the rest of the trip home, they rode without talking. And as they got close to Marianna, the solution to the problem of what to say to Anne came to him. It was a perfect solution, one that solved the problem once and for all.

He would say nothing whatever to Anne. He wouldn't talk to her or see her ever again.

And if Rufus ran at the Bainbridge Track, he would learn he was in a race.

_____ Eleven

I<small>F DAVE WADE</small> had been in charge, he would have stripped the chassis of the wrecked Motor Enterprises Special down to the frame before junking it. There were springs and bolts and fastenings and shock absorbers and vibration dampers and brake fittings and hydraulic lines and fuel lines and mechanical fittings all in good shape, all usable, all worth money.

But Dave Wade was not in charge. He was, as Charley said, vice president for stopping and going. Roger Chedister was in overall charge. And, without a moment's indecision, Roger ordered the whole wrecked car off to the junk yard.

It would cost more money in terms of lost man hours to attempt to salvage parts from the wrecked car than the parts were worth. And, of course, there was no telling when, if ever, they would need, for example, a front, left, brake line.

"Dave, when you haul it out there, you better take a

torch and cut the frame at least once," he said. He said it politely and courteously, but it was unmistakably an order and not a suggestion.

Dave understood the reason for the cutting. Once cut, the car would not run again. No one could give the frame a hit-and-miss straightening, bolt in a transmission, straighten the skin, or body, and put it back on the track.

But still, as he stood with the welder's mask pushed up on his forehead and adjusted the oxygen and acetylene flame until it was just the right blue-white color for cutting he was almost sad.

The frame resisted the torch. It was good, solid steel. Dave had a quick mental image of himself as a twentieth-century version of a cowboy shooting a horse with a broken leg. Instead of a single action Colt .44-40, he had a National Welding Equipment Master Craftsman torch, but the idea was the same.

This was not, he realized, what he had in mind when he came to Florida for the summer. That had been a great deal less complicated, a great deal smaller in scope, and, probably most important, that had been what he was going to do alone. He had not planned to be a one-fourth partner who sensed that if he had to call a vote, he would find himself in a minority of one.

When he thought about it now, as he watched the metal change color and glow and spit and then turn fluid and separate, it was as simple as any of his other childhood dreams. He used to dream of having a horse. He would ride the horse over the fields. He did not consider, of course, that horses had to be housed and fed, and that he owned no fields and didn't know anyone who did.

He had thought he would come South and fix the old car and drive. He had not considered that cars require shops for maintenance, and the automotive equivalent of hay and oats, and the racing equivalent of the fields over which he had in his imagination raced his imaginary horse.

He was through the frame on the driver's side now. A quarter-of-an-inch separated the steel of the frame. Without turning the torch off, he dragged the hoses around to the other side and applied the flame.

He told himself that he really wasn't that stupid. He hadn't made detailed plans for what he would do, because he didn't know what he would find when he got here. He knew that he would have to have help, and he would have arranged for that somehow. He hadn't considered help of the quality of Charley. He had, without consciously thinking about it, expected to have someone with less skill to help him to, for example, make the runs to the local junkyards as Charley had him doing.

He had not considered, even wishfully, getting involved with a Grand National car. That was something that might possibly happen in the distant future, with college over and done with, when he had a great deal of experience behind the wheel of less powerful, much slower cars, raced on smaller and slower tracks. When, Dave realized, he was grown-up.

When he really thought about it, that's what had happened. He had been acting as if he were full-grown and a man, because he liked to be treated like a man. His bluff had been called. He was being treated like a man, and it wasn't quite as he thought it would be. He had never hidden behind the 'teen-ager' or 'young man' label, and had held those who did in scorn, but at home, he was a nice kid and treated like one. There were certain privileges that went with it.

Not privileges, immunities. As diplomats are given in foreign countries. The immunites were gone now. His challenge had been accepted. He wanted to race cars? O.K. But nice kids and nice young men didn't race cars. Men raced cars.

He was through the frame on the passenger side now. The car didn't sag. It smoldered a little, but there was little danger of fire, for the gasoline had been drained from it. One had to look close to see that the frame had been cut. It would, if it were moved, slowly settle, not fall apart, as the weight bent the lighter steel of the body.

Dave shut off the torch, wrapped the double rubber hoses carefully on the cart which held the heavy tanks, and then, with an effort, rolled it back to the old house-trailer serving as office for the junkyard.

He thanked the man in charge, who puffed at an unlit cigar butt and nodded, but didn't speak. Then he went out to the pizza wagon and drove away. He did not allow himself the sentimental gesture of looking back.

The pizza wagon was going to stay. It had been brought up as a matter to be resolved between them. It stayed, not because of any sentimental reason, but for the reason it had appealed to Dave in the North. It met requirements for a trailer-tower and parts van. But Luigi's Neapolitan Pizza was going to have to go.

"On the way back, Dave, drop the truck off at the other place," Roger said. "Comer says he can run it through the paint shop this afternoon."

"Check," Dave had said, and then he emptied the back of the truck while Roger and Charley bent over engineering data for the engines they would rebuild. Dave felt very much as he had felt when he was fourteen, hanging around Wilson's Super Service. He felt that he was just barely being tolerated. It was necessary for him to remind himself that all the effort, even cleaning out the back of the pizza wagon, was toward one end: to put *him* behind the wheel of a very fast automobile to earn prize money to pay for all the time and money and effort they were spending.

They were expecting him at the showroom-garage. The shop foreman waved and gestured for him to drive almost through the shop to the paint section. He had no sooner stopped and shut off the engine when two of the mechanics, who had apparently been taking a coke break, walked up.

"Everything you need out of it, Dave?" one of them asked. Dave was embarrassed that he had forgotten the man's name.

"I think so," Dave said, "but if you find any hundred dollar bills, they're mine."

"Sure," the shop foreman said, smiling.

"Can somebody run me back to the other place?" Dave asked.

"There's your car," the foreman said, nodding toward the convertible Chrysler. His voice revealed a certain confusion, for the car should have been as obvious to Dave Wade as it was to him.

"That belongs in the showroom, doesn't it?" Dave asked.

"No," the foreman said, and again his voice reflected his thinking. It was relieved now. There was an explanation for Dave's apparently unexplainable confusion. "The new showroom queen came in on the same trailer as the Fury," he said. "Bright red with a black top." He paused and thought a moment. "I like this one better though. Don't ask me why."

There were a number of possibilities. It may simply have been time to change the showroom queen, that ultra-fancy model loaded with pizazz that attracted customers like the old candle and the moths. It might simply have been time to sell the old queen. And of course, there was the business of the malted-milk-soiled upholstery.

But what really had happened, Dave knew, was that Comer was giving him a fancy convertible to drive. It made Dave a little uneasy. He tried to tell himself that only the loosest kind of a nut could feel sorry for himself for having exchanged a new Chrysler convertible for an old Studebaker, but that's the way it was.

Comer was being as good as he knew how to be, and Dave was repaying his affection by getting tossed in jail and embarrassing everyone.

Even as he exchanged smiles with the shop foreman, he knew there was absolutely nothing he could do now, but take the Chrysler and take it with a big smile, as if it didn't make him feel like the worst kind of a parasite.

When he got behind the wheel of the Chrysler and looked for the malted-milk damage, it was hard to find. The magic cleanser, he realized, was as advertised. It took a careful stare to find even the suggestion of a stain.

There was nothing wrong with this car. It could serve perfectly as the customer impresser.

He got to the old showroom just as the tractor-trailer, the automobile pullman, was backing up to the door. The driver must have taken time out for lunch on his trip from the new showroom.

Charley and Roger were standing in the doorway, waiting for the driver to stop. Roger waved one hand at Dave, but his attention was on the Fury, the only passenger on the eight-car trailer.

It was white. There was probably some other name for the color, some copy-writer's solemn flight of imagination, like Beach Tan or Arctic Ice or the like, but the Fury was almost pure white. For a car just hauled down the highway, it was unusually clean. Most of the time, new cars arrived covered with grime, dust, and even mud and water splotches. This car was clean.

"There it sits," Roger said, walking over to Dave as Dave closed the door of the convertible. "What do you think?"

"It's pretty," Dave said, for that was what he had been thinking.

"I was hoping for something more profound," Roger said, half-joking. "Such as 'it's a well-engineered chassis.'

Or, 'fine, basic engine design.' "

"You don't think it's pretty?" Dave asked.

"I do, but I'm trying to tell you there's a good excuse for what we're going to have to do to it."

"Which one of you guys is David Wade?" the driver asked.

"I am."

"Sign here," he said, passing over a clipboard and a shipping manifest. "Or do you want to wait until you can eyeball it."

"For what?" Dave asked.

"Well, you know. For the insurance. Maybe the upholstery or the headliner is torn. Or there's a scratch in the paint. Or a dented hubcap or something. You know."

"Under the circumstances," Roger Chedister said, "A dented hubcap would annoy me as much as a determined mosquito working on the hindquarters of an elephant."

He jumped up on the chassis and walked its length so that he was under the Fury, which rode on the top level of the two-level truck.

"What's with him?" the driver asked as Dave handed the signed receipt back to him.

"He's a little odd," Dave said. "Ever since he fell on his head. You know."

"Oh."

"You're the stop and go in this business," Charley said to Dave, not quite able to conceal a smile as the truck driver examined Roger curiously. "Hop to it."

"Keys are in it," the truck driver said. "Taped to the

speedometer."

"Thanks."

Dave climbed into the trailer, and into the car itself as Charley and the truck driver unfolded the pierced steel ramp, and put the supporting braces in place.

The car had a sheet of polyethylene over the upholstery, and thick squares of cardboard on the floor board. FOR PROTECTION UNTIL DELIVERY, they said. He wound the window on his side down, sniffing the peculiar, delightful smell of a new car. Then he jerked the masking tape which held the keys to the glass of the speedometer. Beneath the tape, the odometer read six-tenths of a mile.

"Any time, Dave," Roger called up to him.

Dave took the shiny new keys, put them in the ignition lock, and turned. The engine caught instantly. When Dave tapped the accelerator, the torque of the engine twisted the car on its suspension. He thought, this has got a lot of power. It'll go like a scared rabbit.

Then he reconsidered this.

When Dave and Charley got through doing what they were going to do with this automobile, going like a scared rabbit would be a very inexact simile. It would go like an angry leopard. It would roar and it would snort fire. It would go like an infuriated dragon.

Fury was an appropriate name.

He moved the stiff new shift lever into reverse and very carefully backed off the car pullman. The brakes were so new they squeaked.

As soon as he was off the trailer, Charley got behind him

and guided him with hand signals showing precisely where he wanted the car parked. As Dave turned off the motor, he saw that the odometer had moved from six-tenths of a mile to seven-tenths of a mile. He thought that they were probably going to set some sort of record for the least mileage of any new car before complete rebuilding. One-tenth of a mile. Not even that, really. The odometer had been ready to turn over when he started the engine.

When he got out, Roger was helping the truck driver store the pierced steel ramp. Dave turned and looked at the car. From the engine compartment came the faint smell of burning paint. This car was so very new.

Roger came into the building and closed the door. He looked at the car.

"I guess this will go quicker if I help Charley, Dave," he said. "Do you want to strip it inside?"

"Sure," Dave said.

"Let's get it up on blocks first," Charley said. "I think it'll save us time in the long run."

They weren't really blocks. They were of heavy steel, and there were six of them placed with great care under the frame so that the car was firmly supported, and also so that two of the supports could be removed, when necessary, to get at different parts of the undercarriage.

With the blocks in place, the car did not move when Dave opened the door and climbed inside. He thought of this, and he took a little pleasure in it. This was what kids in gas stations, or in their own garages, toying with carburetors, adjusting again and again spark plug gaps, doing any of the hundred things they could do, and telling themselves they were making their cars run faster, or smoother, or more economically, dreamed of doing.

This was professional. There would be no cut corners here, no philosophy of 'it'll do, I hope.' Everything from here on, literally from the ground up, would be professional and first class.

He was sitting behind the wheel. What to do first?

"Trip the hood, Dave," Charley called, and Dave pulled the hood release-lever. Charley bent over the car, but not over the engine. With a crescent wrench, he attacked the bolts that held the hood to the fire wall. There was a creaking sound, and the bolt began to turn. The stripping was underway. Dave was pleased, somehow, that Charley had started the tearing-down process.

Then he shook himself from his lassitude, got out of the car, and pulled the new seat from the seat frame on the floor. He carried it to the side of the work area and put it on the floor against the wall. When he returned to the car, he began to unfasten the bolts which held the seat bottom to the floor board.

The three of them were going to take apart what a large number of highly paid technicians had spent a great many hours putting together. And just about everything would go.

It seemed a shame that so much was being wasted. It would obviously have been easier all the way around if the factory had not installed the seats, upholstery, headliners, headlights, and parking lights.

But the Chrysler Corporation was not in racing. It was not in the business of selling racing cars or even cars designed for racing. It could not stop anyone from racing one of its automobiles once he had bought it, any more than it would have had the right to keep someone from repainting the car in purple and chartreuse polka dots. But it would not assist in any way, and Chrysler considered that selling a car that could be more easily adapted for racing was assisting.

Dave understood Chrysler's reasoning, but there was still something basically wrong in what they were doing, because waste is basically wrong. He knew that what they took out of this car, the seats, the side panels, the headliner, the headlights and even the steering wheel would go into Comer's part room, where, it was possible but not probable, they would be used. For ethical reasons, they could only be used on cars Comer owned, for they were used parts simply because they had been installed, and despite the fact they were really quite new.

If Comer had a wrecked car that needed parts he could use these. Otherwise, there was a very good chance that they would lie on the shelf for years, until they were thrown away because they were cluttering up the place.

Dave unbolted the seat base, and took that out, and then crawled further into the car, removing the rear seat cushion, the base, and the back. With this gone, he could begin to unscrew the interior panels, first in back, and then on the doors.

Once he started to work the time passed quickly. He was

awakened from his concentration by a delightful smell of warm hamburgers, fried onions, and toasted roll. His stomach constricted. It was of the greatest importance that he eat and eat now.

He had been bent over in what had been the back seat, working with a Phillips screwdriver on a catch that held taillight wiring in place. When he straightened up, he found himself facing a broadly smiling Roger, who was waving an unwrapped hamburger back and forth.

"I thought that would bring you to life," he said. "Tell me, Friend, could I interest you in some food for the stomach?"

Dave was twice delighted. First with the food (and the fact that Roger had bought enough so that he wouldn't feel like a hog when he ate four hamburgers) and then with Roger himself, for going for the hamburgers and milk, and not sending Dave, like the errand boy Dave had begun to consider himself.

They ate standing up, leaning against the car. Dave saw that the engine had been stripped. The alternator, carburetor, and even the intake manifold had been unbolted and put to one side. Parts that might be used (such as the intake manifold and the alternator) were in one stack, and parts that had no place in a racing car (window washer and its hoses and tank, the windshield wipers and their hoses) in another.

He completely enjoyed his lunch. He was honestly hungry after his hard work, and he was in the company of friends. Even as Dave thought of this, he knew that while he could never say it to either Charley or Roger, he didn't have to say it. He sensed somehow that they already knew.

They balled up the waxed paper and milk cartons and tossed them into the 55-gallon drum used as a wastebasket. Then they went back to work.

The next time Dave became aware of the time it was quarter to six, and Roger was pulling at his foot.

"Come on, ambitious," Roger said. "Enough's enough! All work and no play and similar profound thoughts."

"I've got two more bolts and we can get the whole dashboard out," Dave said, his voice from behind the dashboard sounded as if he were in a barrel.

"Two bolts will hold until morning," Roger said. "We've had a good day."

He tugged again at Dave's feet. He was joking, but Dave considered that it was entirely possible that Roger would haul him out bodily unless he came voluntarily and immediately.

Dave came out from behind the dashboard and rested a moment, sitting on the floor where the front seat had been. The interior was stripped. The car was a hollow shell. It looked naked and even unpleasant with the upholstery and headliner gone. There was a marked contrast because he had not removed the tire cover and other upholstery in the trunk, but had removed the cardboard between the passenger compartment and the trunk itself.

"Good day's work," Roger said. "We can pull the engine and the transmission tomorrow, and maybe the suspension too."

"I'm tired," Dave said.

"Too tired to do something new for a change?"

"Such as?"

"I thought maybe we could run down to the Bay Track at Pensacola. Some of the people you're running against Wednesday in the old car are running tonight."

"I'd like to see that," Dave said. "I've got to go home for dinner, though, or my aunt will have a fit. I'd like to ask you, Roger, but . . ."

"Comer already has," Roger said. "And I've accepted with pleasure. As a matter of fact, I'm moving in with you-all."

"You are?"

"Comer says that if I'm there, Marge won't be able to regard me as such an evil influence on you. Besides, that boarding house room wasn't what you could call really comfortable on these summer nights."

"I hadn't thought about that," Dave thought aloud. "Are you just going to stay here? Aren't you going home?"

"Atlanta's kind of far, if you want to commute," Roger said. "I've got to be here."

"I guess so," Dave said. But then he realized that Roger was really saying more than this. He was making it official that this was all business, making it official that he was investing a great deal more than some loose money and some free time. He was putting all of his time into this, and that meant all of his money too.

And he thought again that Comer was really a good guy. Whether he was taking Roger into the house because he was Dave's friend or because he was a partner was not important. What was important was that he was taking him in and sparing him the loneliness of a rooming house.

"And if you ask me very politely," Roger said, with a perfectly solemn face, "I'll even ride in that roofless automobile of yours."

Dave looked at Roger for a full thirty seconds, trying to think of something, anything, to say to that. When he could think of nothing whatever to reply, he shrugged his shoulders and walked out to the car. Roger ran ahead of him, opened the driver's door, and with mock elegance, bowed as Dave got in behind the wheel. Then he ran around the other side and jumped inside. Suddenly, he snapped his fingers and the smile vanished. "Dave, I forgot to tell you something important," he said.

"What's that, Roger?" Dave asked.

"The long, thin thing on the right makes it go," Roger said very seriously, "and the short, squarish one on the left makes it stop. Think you can remember all that?"

"I think so," Dave said.

"See if you can stay on the black stuff between the trees," Roger suggested helpfully.

"I'll try," Dave said, and then he laughed. Roger looked at him and raised one eyebrow.

"Never forget, young man, that it is much easier to go around trees than through them," Roger said. "Let that be the guiding principle of your career."

"As vice-president in charge of stop and go?"

"That's clever. Don't tell me you thought that up all by

yourself?"

"Charley said it."

"Rather apt," Roger said. Dave fastened the seat belt, and then released the parking brake and moved onto the street. "There's a great deal more to Charley than meets the eye."

There's a great deal more to you than meets the eye, Dave thought.

_____ Twelve

By THE TIME it was time for the main event at Bainbridge, Dave Wade was very tired and very dirty. It was his fourth race of the night. Despite what Lou Watters, who owned the track, had promised (and, oddly enough, despite the fact that Watters had practically greeted them at the track entrance with a certified check for the $250 starting money) Dave had had to run in the novice race.

He didn't enter it to win by a country mile. There was no point in risking damage to even the old Ford to win the novice race. He entered it to qualify to race for the larger prize money. He went around and around and around, ten times in all, starting near the tail of the pack, working his way up slowly and steadily as others fell out. There were two drivers in the pack of twenty that had, he thought, no business being on the public highways, much less a race track. They apparently believed that the key to racing success was a lead foot heavily applied to the accelerator. They came to a time of reckoning before the second lap was over. One spun out on the far turn, careened off the outside retaining wall, and stopped, facing the wrong direction. The second lost control during a slide on the near turn, kept sliding, and was struck broadside by the following car.

In the instant in which this happened, Dave had gotten a glimpse of the face of the driver of the following car. He was obviously standing on the binders, but the binders weren't going to help. His face showed both horror and surprise that this was really happening to him.

Four cars went out for mechanical failure, one spectacularly when an apparently ruptured fuel tank sprayed gasoline on the exhaust pipe. The gasoline burst into flame, and a dense cloud of black smoke appeared. The other mechanical failures were less spectacular. One car lost a front wheel going into the start-finish straightaway, and ground to an embarrassing, though not dangerous, halt right in front of the spectators. And two starters simply stopped going. There was no way to tell what had happened to them. They could have lost oil pressure, and the engines could have frozen; they could have lost fuel pumps, or generators, or gears, or any one of the hundred things necessary to keep a car going.

Dave did not drive to lose, either. When the opportunity came he dropped his foot a bit heavier on the accelerator, or waited one extra second before removing pressure and shifting down.

When the ten laps were over, he was third car to take the checkered flag. Prize money was $25. They had figured they must have a return of $300 to break even for the night's racing. With the starting money and this $25, they were $25 shy of that. If he could place in either of the secondary events, which would bring $50 prize, without wrecking the car, they would come out $25 ahead.

He went out to qualify for the next race as soon as Charley had tried the tires and the engine, and Roger had gassed it up and thrown in a quart of oil. He drove faster now, against the clock, shaving the corners closely, controlling the slides, working the gearbox with quick, almost savage movements. Three seemed to be his number tonight. He was third fastest in time and he was given starting spot number three on the starting grid, which meant that he was outside in the front row.

The old Ford had a lot of power and a lot of torque. It wasn't the most attractive car running, but it was probably the best prepared and the guttiest. He took first place in the second race simply by roaring to an immediate lead, using his superior acceleration from a stop, and then staying there. The man on his tail had, on purpose Dave felt, slid into him taking a corner. There was a sound of crushed metal and a loss of feel in the steering wheel as the end was pushed out. For an instant something sour rose from Dave's stomach and tasted foul in his mouth.

He whipped the wheel two inches to the right, increasing the arc of his slide, and then, foot jammed to the floor, back to the left. The engine seemed to hesitate for a second, then the wheels dug in. Dave shot ahead of the car, ran parallel to it until there were two full car lengths between them, and then cut left in front of him as he entered the far curve. He stayed at least a full car-length ahead until the checkered flag was waved at him.

He took the victory lap without looking at the stands, feeling a little embarrassed. Then he pulled into the pits.

First prize money was $125. They were ahead $100 for the evening with all expenses paid.

"Shall we quit while we're ahead?" Roger asked, as he handed Dave the coke bottle full of water.

"Let's keep trying."

Roger nodded. "I don't think he hurt you," he said. "Little body damage. A little game of wrinkle fender. I don't think he expected your guts."

Dave looked at him.

"The engine's guts," Roger said in clarification. "Although you weren't exactly a pantywaist out there, old Buddy."

"I'm going to wash some of this crud off my face," Dave said. "I'm not in the next one, am I?"

"Next one's invitational. Your buddy is in it."

"What?"

"Battling Rufus," Roger said. "Old One-Two-Punch himself."

"Let that be a lesson to you, Roger," Dave said, not as embarrassed as he expected to be by a reminder of his defeat. "Never slug someone bigger than you."

Roger chuckled and reached for the gas cap.

Dave wondered why he was surprised that Rufus was there. He had known that he was going to be there. Immediately after he had found himself sitting on the gravel in the drive-in parking lot, he had vowed that he would beat him soundly, like Sir Galahad defeating the Bad and Wicked Knight for the hand of the fair maiden.

David, he told himself, you don't belong here. You belong in the basement of St. Michael's Church, trying to make a bonfire by rubbing two sticks together with the rest of the twelve-year-old boy scouts.

He washed his face, but it didn't do much good. There was no hot water and the layer of grease and burned oil and rubber could not be removed. It made him feel a little better, however. He rubbed his face vigorously with the towel.

When he straightened up, a young man was looking at him.

"You're Wade?"

"Uh huh."

"Hard feelings?"

"For what?"

"I hit you in the left tail."

"Oh," Dave said, and looked at him. "No. I'm not sore."

"I thought you'd give way," the young man said. "I'll know better the next time."

"I didn't think you'd hit me," Dave said. "I'll know better next time."

"Fair enough," the young man said. "I'm Dave Stevens. Can I buy you a coke?"

Dave put out his hand. "That's a fine first name you have, Dave Stevens," he said. "I'll be honored to have a coke with you."

The paddock here was open to the public. The pits themselves, of course, were restricted to drivers and crews, but
the paddock was full of people who wanted to be closer to
the cars and drivers than they could get in the grandstands.

"How about a hot dog?" Dave Stevens asked, and Dave
Wade nodded pleased acceptance.

"Two all the way, and two cokes, large ones," Stevens
said.

A man Dave had never seen before in his life grabbed his
hand and shook it violently, "Fine race, Dave. Really
showed your stuff."

"Thank you," Dave said. He flushed.

The man pounded him three times, heavily, on the back,
beamed at him again, and vanished in the crowd.

Dave Stevens smiled.

"First time that's happened?" he asked over his shoulder
as he reached for the coke bottles.

"Does it happen often?"

"If you win, it happens often," Stevens said. He handed
Dave a coke. "They like winners. I guess you could say
that's a rule of life." He turned again and took the hot dogs
which were in little cardboard boats, wrapped in thin waxed
paper. He handed Dave one and turned with a bill in his
hand to pay for them.

The white-capped counter clerk shook his head and nodded and then pointed to a smiling man in his forties. The
man, when Dave and Dave looked at him, waved. Dave
Stevens waved back, and, without moving his lips, said,

"Wave, Dave."

Feeling very foolish, Dave raised his hand, forced a smile and waved.

"I'd just as soon buy my own hot dog," he said.

"So would I," Dave Stevens said. "But if you refused the free coke and the free hot dog, you'd hurt that guy's feelings. He gets sort of a thrill from it. He'll probably go home and tell the boys at the gas station about what you said—or I said—when we were all having a coke together. It doesn't do any harm, Dave. It's part of this business. There's more to it than making a car go fast, you know. We're performers. My professor of psychology says we're the gladiators of the Twentieth Century."

"Your professor of psychology?" Dave asked.

"I've got one year to go. Georgia Tech. Major in metallurgy. Minor in psychology. That's quite a combination."

"I've got two years to go," Dave said. This was the first time he'd thought of this since coming to Florida. "I'm in engineering, with a minor in pre-law. I still have time to change."

"That's surprising," Dave Stevens said. "There's not much need for lawyers in this business. We have sort of an unwritten law that we don't take each other to court for what happens out there." He nodded at the track.

"I don't know if I can make it in this business," Dave said. "It's still fairly new to me."

"Are you trying to tell me that you don't have much driving experience?" Stevens asked.

"Very little, as a matter of fact," Dave admitted.

"Then have no fear, Friend. You can make it all right."

They didn't say anything else, but finished the hot dogs and the cokes, and then wordlessly started back to the pits. Dave Wade could see that Dave Stevens was smiling and waving at a large number of people, and that their smiles, tentative and embarassed at first, grew warm and pleased when Stevens replied to them. He found that it worked for him, too. A tough-looking character in a leather jacket, with a crew cut, crooked teeth, and the suggestion of a smile on his face, raised his hand in a faint gesture of salute. Dave knew that the man was afraid his gesture of recognition and friendship would be rebuffed.

Dave smiled, winked, and raised his hand. "How goes it?" he asked.

"You take that main event, you hear?" the man said, and his smile was full now, and he didn't look nearly so rough and forbidding.

"I'll try," Dave said.

Fifty yards farther, Dave Stevens said, "See what I mean?"

"Yeah."

"I'll see you around, Dave," Stevens said and put out his hand.

"Thanks for the coke and hot dog," Dave said.

"Don't thank me," Stevens said. He gestured with his hand and smiled.

Then he turned and walked toward his pit.

When Dave got back to his pit, Comer was there, and he and Charley and Roger were waiting.

"The way you're running out there, Dave," Roger began without preliminaries, "I decided it would be best to put in some cold plugs and to fill the gas tank. That'll put a little more weight on the rear wheels, so I put fresh rubber on the front. I don't think you'll have much of a change in handling characteristics, but to be on the safe side, you'd better take it easy the first couple of laps."

Dave nodded but didn't reply. He paid attention, of course, but what Stevens had said about college was in his mind. He did not, certainly, still belong in the Boy Scouts. But he did belong in a classroom. He wondered if he really belonged here, at a race track, where people bought him hot dogs and cokes because he was a winner.

Charley wanted to take a look at the gear shift linkage, and Dave nodded in agreement without really understanding what he was saying. He rubbed his eyes, which still tickled where the goggle nosepiece rested. When he looked up, he looked across the track into the grandstand, into the faces of people sitting and eating popcorn and hot dogs, drinking cokes, and waiting for the Roman games to begin again.

He found himself looking into the blue eyes of Anne Wagner. She met his eyes for a minute and then they both looked away.

"Dave?" Roger said, a little annoyed.

"Sorry, I was thinking."

"Did you get something to drink when you were gone?"

"I had a coke and a hot dog."

"You better take some more water. Or coke, if you want.

If you don't watch yourself, the way you sweat, you actually get dehydrated and your reflexes slow up."

"O.K.," Dave said, and drained another coke bottle full of water. Then he got behind the wheel and polished his goggles with a Kleenex while Roger and Comer strapped him in. Charley made one last, final adujstment to the carburetor.

The competition was stiff in the race before the main event. There were drivers who had not previously qualified the main event and were determined to do so now. The second and third place winners of the novice race, flushed with recent proof of their own skill were determined to prove it again.

Dave was learning difference between a determination to win, and a desperation to win. A driver became desperate to win when he absolutely had to have the prize money. When he had to have it, he would take chances, either in driving or in pushing the car beyond its limits. When that happened, the desperate driver became a menace to himself and to the other cars on the track.

But there was no way to tell who was desperate and who was simply determined. On the other side of the coin, there was no way that anyone could tell about people like Dave, who would race to win but would not take dangerous and even suicidal chances to win.

There was a cold, unpleasant logical conclusion to be drawn from all this. As the size of the prize money went up, so did the quality of the drivers and the safety of the cars. The greater danger in racing was at the small track with worn out cars being raced for small amounts of money by desperate drivers.

In the race before the main event, the 1950 Ford coupe, owned by Motor Enterprises and driven by David Wade, placed sixth in a finishing field of eighteen cars. Wade won $37.50 in lap money, three laps at $12.50 per lap. His speed was 58.133 mph for the course, comparing with 62.010 mph of the winner.

In the time trials which immediately followed, Wade ran 64.340 mph, which gave him the number two spot on the starting grid behind Lester Hollans, who drove a '55 Plymouth at 65.550 and in front of Jerry Kroller, driving a '60 Chevie at 63.960.

The main event was fifty laps or twenty-five miles, and there were twenty-four entries. That meant that cars were three abreast and eight deep on the starting grid. Conversation was impossible during that last minute before the checkered flag whipped down, and the rising and falling sound of raced engines became an angry howl, broken only as the cars searched for position and found it was necessary to slow and accelerate.

Dave hit the flag perfectly. He had just the right amount of engine speed and clutch engagement to get him moving quickly, but without laying rubber and when he went up into second the tach barely dipped before it began to climb again. It was, beyond a doubt, the finest racing start he had ever made.

It put him third into the first turn, behind the number one grid starter and the number four grid starter, and barely ahead of number two. It was a quick and brutal lesson. He was no longer going to be able to coast a little because the old Ford had more guts than the competition.

He went into third gear in the second he was out of the drift and onto the rear straightaway, and here the engine-gear ratio worked to his advantage. He pulled into second place, but found when he had to go down in the gears for the far turn that he couldn't hold it. Number four starter, a '53 Ford coupe, nosed him out, and Dave had to fall back into number three spot again.

And they went around and around this way, and after the fourth attempt to take and, most important, keep, second place, Dave resigned himself to the knowledge that he wasn't going to get it unless something else happened. He turned his concentration to the next most important thing, keeping his third place spot against the fourth place holder, who wanted it badly, and, to judge by qualifying speed, had the guts to take it the second he could take advantage of any mistake of Dave's.

Although it was the longest race Dave had ever entered, it was over more quickly than any of the others had been. It was over very much the way it began for Dave, in third place, although the first car to take the checkered flag was the '53 Ford coupe which slid into a turn halfway through the race and nosed out the '55 Plymouth for first place.

Dave had had no reasonable chance to do better. He was disappointed, but not angry with himself or with anything else. It had been a good race.

He could take a great deal of consolation in third place

money. Number one had been worth $750, number two $500, and the number three $250. There would be no red ink on the ledger for tonight.

"I knew you'd confuse the stop and go pedals," Roger said when he coasted into the pits and shut off the engine. But he was smiling, and when Dave got out of the car, Roger punched him on the arm, in the almost universal gesture of friendship between men.

"The board of directors has just voted to buy us all a steak," Comer said, "and we'll take you with us, if you figure you can scrape some of that muck off your face."

"I'll give it a whirl," Dave said. He felt happy and relaxed, and when, in the men's room, he met Dave Stevens, they shook hands again.

"Good race, Dave," Stevens said. "I didn't have a chance to get out of the hole. The rest of us were just along for the ride."

When he came out of the men's room, he saw Rufus, who looked at him, but didn't speak.

"Friend of yours, Dave?" Stevens asked.

"I took a poke at him, and he knocked me on my taillights," Dave heard himself admitting.

"Really?" Stevens said, and smiled. "Well, you made up for it today. He couldn't even get around me, much less around you. I guess he finished twentieth."

"Would you think I was a poor winner if I said that it didn't really break my heart, and I don't think I'll lose any sleep over it at all?"

"Not at all. Just between you, me, and the world, Dave,

Rufus is one of the people I like to beat."

And then, with a casual wave, Dave Stevens was gone. It didn't seem necessary that they say good-bye or that they would see one another soon again; this seemed to be mutually understood.

When he got back to the pits, the old Ford was already on the trailer behind the pizza wagon, and Charley was already behind the wheel.

"There's a good place to get a steak at the Holiday Inn," Roger shouted. "We'll see you there." Charley nodded his agreement, and the pizza wagon, now advertisementless, bounced out of the pit.

They waited for Comer, who arrived with a smile on his face and half-a-dozen checks in his hand.

"The older I get," he said, "the more I agree that these are prettier than a female."

"Why not one check?"

"Good idea, really. They make them out as you earn them, after each race. That way, there's only a little waiting when the meet is over. You've got a standing offer of two fifty for starting money, Dave. Once a month, if you want it."

"We'll think about it," Roger said, reminding Dave that these decisions were no longer his alone to make.

The restaurant in the motel was full. In luxurious, and, more important, very clean, surroundings, Dave was painfully aware that he had managed only to scrape the surface of the dirt from his face and hands. He headed again for the men's room, where, certainly, there would be hot water.

When he got to the table, they had ordered for him. Comer had told the waitress to just leave the pitcher of ice tea on the table; they would drink it all. He had just taken an envelope of sugar and torn it open when Anne Wagner said, "Congratulations, Dave."

He looked up and saw her. She was with Rufus and some others he vaguely recognized, but whom he knew must be Rufus' pit crew. There was another girl and three other men. The hostess, seeing that they knew each other, seated them at an adjacent table.

"Thank you," Dave said, getting to his feet.

"Yeah, Wade," Rufus said. "Congratulations. Pity you didn't have more experience. That's quite a car, that old Ford."

Dave felt his face flush again. But he didn't lose his temper.

"How did you do, Rufus?" he asked, forcing himself to smile.

"Ah, the old bucket's worn out," Rufus said. "It wouldn't go. I did pretty bad."

"That's a shame," Dave said, and now it was his turn. "How bad?"

"Twentieth," Rufus said, forcing a smile on his face.

"You think that was the difference, Rufus?" Roger asked softly. "You mean, for example, if you and Dave had swapped cars, you'd have done better?"

"That's what I mean," Rufus said, and even he must have sensed that it sounded arrogant for he tried to soften it. "After all," he said. "There aren't many cars like that

[177]

around, set up by a master like Charley."

Very clever, Rufus, Dave thought. You weaseled out of that very nicely.

Rufus was apparently thinking the same thing, for he went on. "You wouldn't know where I could buy a car like that, would you? I've got to get rid of my worn-out junker. Or I'll never win."

"Are you serious?" Roger asked smoothly.

"Sure. Anytime you want a job, Charley . . ."

"If you're serious, Rufus, I do know," Roger went on.

"Where?" Rufus interrupted. His tone was sarcastic.

"We'll sell you the old Ford," Roger said. "I don't know what it's worth, so we'll have it appraised. How's that?"

No matter what Rufus was thinking, he knew he was trapped.

"O.K.," he said. "You got a deal."

He turned and picked up the menu to show that the conversation was over.

"I wouldn't argue with Rufus, of course," Roger said loudly enough so that everybody at Rufus' table could hear, "but I got the idea that if you'd had another three or four miles an hour, you could have taken that tonight, Dave. But maybe Rufus'll prove me wrong."

Dave could not resist the temptation to see Anne Wagner's reaction to all this. When he looked at her, she was giving him a dirty look. It seemed to Dave that she had chosen sides, and not his.

Thirteen

RUFUS, to Roger's admitted surprise, was good to his word. The old Ford was appraised by a disinterested trio of NASCAR officials, and Rufus wrote out a check on the spot for the full amount.

Dave was a little sorry to see the old Ford go. It had been, really, his first car, for he had been the chief mechanic and not the driver of the original Motor Enterprises Special. But he understood why Roger had been so willing to sell it. The time they devoted to keeping the old Ford in racing trim had to be taken—*stolen*, was the word Roger used—from the new car. Even winning, with the winner's purses, the old car was costing them money in terms of time and attention.

Once they had the Fury stripped to the chassis, they started putting it back together. Where the frame had been spot-welded together (that is, every six or eight inches, it had inch-long arc-welds) it was now fully welded. The stresses of extreme speed, of brutal acceleration and de-celeration required that the frame be three or four times as rigid and strong as it would have had to be for any highway use.

New springs and spring housings were welded in place. Quarter-inch steel was welded between the floor-board and the clutch so that if the clutch should fly apart under the great forces of acceleration, Dave wouldn't be killed by fragments. A roll-bar was welded to the frame. This was heavy steel pipe following the outline of the windshield in the forward upsidedown U. Another inverted U was imme-diately behind the seat. A third piece of piping ran down the center of the car, tying the two U's together and continu-ing rearward to the frame, just in front of the fuel tank.

A bucket seat was installed, and it, too, was welded in place. The steering wheel was covered with black tape to increase friction. The beautiful, tastefully shaped instru-ment panel was replaced with several lengths of L-iron. Di-rectly before Dave's eyes was an outsize tachometer. Beside it were large, easy-to-read gauges giving fuel pressure, oil temperature, water pressure and generator amperage. The gear shift lever stuck its functional head through a second sheet of sheet steel, this one protecting Dave from frag-ments should the transmission explode at very high speeds.

The seat belt and shoulder harness weren't pretty, and they weren't designed for comfort. They were designed to keep Dave in the seat in case of an accident.

Roger Chedister knew that the fire wall of the car, sel-dom even considered by the average motorist, was, at the speeds at which Dave would be racing, what was known aerodynamically as a source of parasitic drag. It was as if a sheet of metal four feet square were held out into the wind stream.

The firewall was torn out, and sheet-metal ducts directed the airflow down and out beside and under the driver's seat. Two large, heavy fire-bottles were installed, one in the trunk, above and immediately behind the fuel tank, and the second where the front seat passenger would have been if the Fury had had normal seats. These, when triggered either by a toggle switch mounted on the L-bar instrument panel or by the force of a sudden stop, would flood the inside of the car with chemical foam to smother fire and protect Dave's life.

The engine had been torn down and rebuilt with almost incredible care. Pistons had been weighed and ground and weighed again, so that there was no more than one-half ounce difference between any two pistons. There was no muffler now, and the engine roared, but this was not simply proof that the mufflers had been left off.

The exhaust system of an engine is a part of the engine. An inefficient exhaust system, one that did not scavenge burned fuel properly would cut down the efficiency of the engine—and the car's speed. The straight pipes finally installed did a great deal more than make a loud noise.

Magnesium wheels, holding oversized racing tires worth $100 each, replaced the stamped steel wheels with which the car had been equipped. Everything that wasn't necessary was stripped; and everything that was necessary was reinforced and strengthened.

They worked eight hours a day, and then, as often as not, five or six hours after supper. It took almost three weeks for the car to be finished. From fifty feet away (unless you saw the roll-bar assembly, and noticed that the headlights had been removed and that the hood fastener was of heavy, foolproof steel), the car didn't look very different from a car in the showroom. The one exception was the tires. They set the car apart from anything that was supposed to run on a highway carrying children to school and women back and forth to the supermarket.

Dave returned from what must have been his fiftieth trip to the railroad station and bus depot for parts to find a sign painter hard at work.

On each door there was now a sign—Dave Wade.

That was all it said, but the sign painter had drawn speed lines on each letter.

"Is that necessary?" Dave asked.

"You think that's bad, do you?" Roger asked.

"I'm not the most modest guy in the world, but I would have been happy to do without that," Dave said.

"Don't go away. Find yourself a chair and sit in it."

Charley was wearing his twisted-lips look that, once you got to know him, was like a neon sign reading: "I'm up to something."

Dave hadn't the foggiest idea what it could be. Finally, somewhat sheepishly, Comer appeared and then Charley, both of them obviously pushed by Roger. All three were wearing yellow and red sateen jackets, so bright they could have been used on the stage. On the right breast were the crossed checkered flags, the long-time racing symbol. On the left breast, it said Comer, Charley, or Roger.

"If you guys want to look like that," Dave said, "be my guests. Just don't expect me to get dressed up like that where people are liable to see me."

Comer looked even more sheepish.

"All at once," Roger said, and then he gave the military command, "About face."

They shuffled so that they were facing away from Dave. On the back of the jacket, in red letters against the yellow material, and superimposed against another checkered flag, the letters spelled out: THE DAVE WADE RACING TEAM.

"Oh, come on," Dave said. "Whose brilliant, idiot idea was this?"

"Mine," Roger said. "It's what they call attracting the customers."

Roger turned around and came up with another jacket. This one, which had yellow where the others had red and red where the others had yellow, didn't say THE DAVE WADE RACING TEAM. It said, simply, in huge letters, superimposed on a checkered flag, DAVE WADE.

"Well, take it," Roger said. "You're liable to get chilly way up north in Darlington, South Carolina."

Dave took it from him, feeling a little ridiculous. "Do I have to?"

"Right."

"When are we going to Darlington?"

"Charley and I are leaving tonight with the pizza wagon and the car. You're going to follow us up in the morning."

"There's probably a reason for that," Dave said. "You've got something you want me to do here, or else we'd all leave tonight."

"I thought you might want to have dinner with your Aunt Marge," Comer said, and Dave felt about three-quarters of an inch tall.

"I'm sorry," he said. Comer just shrugged.

He felt worse when they got home and he saw what Aunt Marge had done for his farewell dinner. It was, he thought, as if he were going on a five-year trip to Jupiter, instead of only to South Carolina for a couple of weeks.

She made a real effort to be cheerful and bright and witty and gay, and the more she did this, the more Dave became convinced that she really loved him, and that he had been something less than a gentleman since he had been here. He had treated her like his mother, and when he thought of this, he remembered having been accused by his mother, with what were probably tears in her eyes, of treating home like a hotel.

His mother, of course, had the other kids. Aunt Marge had had no kids at all. She had looked forward to having him, a young man, a relative, a member of the family, around the house, and he had been around the house only long enough to sleep, bathe, change into clean clothing and stuff his face.

"You know," he said to her, "I really like it down here."

This was true, but he was ashamed of himself for two

reasons. One, for not having said it before, and two for saying it now to make her feel better. This made him feel like a hypocrite. He realized that it was almost a coincidence that he 'liked it down here.'

She smiled warmly, and reached out and touched his hand.

"I'm glad, Dave," she said. "I wish you could be here all the time."

"I've been thinking," he heard himself say, "that I might transfer down to the University of Florida for next year."

He was horrified. That thought had not occurred to him until he heard himself speak it out loud.

"Oh, that would be wonderful," Aunt Marge said. And she squeezed the hand that she had been holding lightly. "You could come home on weekends," she said, and then, after a pause, as if she had considered this remark and decided that she was being possessive, "When you didn't have anything special at college, I mean," she said.

Dave smiled, hoping the smile didn't look as sick as he felt. Comer was obviously as pleased as Aunt Marge. Everything was hunky-dory, First Class, Grade A, Number One, except for the small item. He would have to explain this sudden change in scholastic planning to his mother and his stepfather.

That he thought, as Aunt Marge put another slice of rare roast beef on his plate, was going to be less painful to think about than it would be to talk about, and it was very painful to think about.

On the way out of Marianna the next morning, heading

South on U.S. 90, David Wade, driving a new Chrysler convertible with money in his pocket, en route to take the wheel of a Grand National racing car at a major racing track, felt that he was in trouble over his head. No matter what he did, he was bound to cause some sort of trouble, hurt someone's feelings.

All I have to do now, he thought, is run the Fury into a brick wall so I lose everyone's money, as well as everyone's confidence and trust.

He soon found, when he got to Darlington, when he got to Grand National Racing, that it was a great deal different from dirt-track, or secondary-track, racing. This was all business, all seriousness, all professionalism.

He was required to take another physical examination, head to toe, a tough, probing, three-hour exam that included an electrocardiogram, and tests of his peripheral vision and hearing. When it was over, the doctor told him that he gave almost exactly the same physical examination to commercial pilots.

The Fury was checked by a full-time (rather than volunteer) examiner. That took the better part of a morning, and, before it was over, Dave, judging by the scowling official, was becoming convinced that they would be told to take their car and go home.

But the Fury passed. A decal was stuck to the inside of the door. This car was safe on the track. The next question was whether or not the proposed driver could be allowed on the track, to race at speeds in excess of 150 miles an hour against other professionals.

A committee of three drivers was named. If they decided that Dave could race, he could race. If they decided that he would be a hazard on the track—not only to himself but to others—he would not be allowed on the track. It was as simple and as blunt as that.

Dave met them at the track at a quarter-past seven on a Thursday morning. He had been so nervous that he hadn't eaten. They were friendly men, but not cordial, not back-slappers. This wasn't a fraternity initiation in college, Dave realized painfully, but, rather, a professional examination. This was for keeps.

They drank a cup of coffee together, and they chatted with him. Dave was not so naive as to confuse the polite conversation with casual conversation. They deftly probed his background, checked his mechanical knowledge, got his viewpoints on driving, on automobile racing generally, and on life itself.

Without being rude, they managed to let him know that they thought he was very young to be entering Grand National racing, and that they had sincere, professional, and deep-seated doubt concerning his professional ability.

Then they went out with him to the car, and, behind a police veil of courteous interest, found out exactly how much he knew about the car in which he proposed to race. Mechanically, Dave felt that he was on solid ground. He knew the parts and what they were designed to do. But he was fully aware that his mechanical knowledge was nothing more than a theoretical knowledge. He knew, for example, that his compression ratio was about 11.5:1. He knew that this expressed the mathematical ratio between the capacity of the cylinder in its opposed placements: at its openmost position, when it ingested the gasoline-air mixture; and at its most closed position, at the moment of ignition.

But this was nothing more, really, than theoretical knowledge. He didn't know how the engine would behave in the middle of a race, or at which point he was most likely to strain the engine beyond its strength. He knew what made disc brakes stop a moving vehicle, and how they were an improvement over the old style binders. Disc brakes, using hydraulic pressure, clamped twin discs against a flat surface. Old style binders forced an abrasive surface outward against a circular brake drum.

But he did not know at what point clamping on the binders would send the Fury into an uncontrollable skid; or how much they would slow a car moving 150 mph before failing. He knew simply that they wouldn't stop a car moving that fast. Nothing would stop a car moving that fast.

These were things a driver sensed. These were things that came with experience, and these were things Dave's trio of friendly inquisitors were almost convinced he could not possibly yet know.

"What we'd like you to do, Dave," the smallest of them said with a gentle smile, "is take a couple of laps. We'd like to see you take her into a couple of slides, and we'd like to see how you handle her generally. Don't try to bust the track lap record. Don't even make a speed run. Take her out for a Sunday drive."

"Yes, sir," Dave said. And he knew that this was another

mistake. Or another indication that he was too young, and that they were right, and he didn't belong here. He had said "Yes, sir," in the same polite, obedient, eager to please tone of voice used by boy scouts replying to their scoutmasters.

One of the committee walked directly across the track, so that he could watch Dave come out of the far bend, go down the straightaway, and enter the rear bend. The second member of the committee, a great big hulk of a man, walked toward a position where he could get the same view on the opposite side of the track. The man who did most of the talking, the perhaps self-appointed chairman, was obviously going to the station himself, in the center of the turn, to watch Dave's handling of the car in the curve.

Charley started the Fury's engine while Dave strapped on his helmet and then began to strap himself into the seat. The engine was cold. It sounded, according to Roger, like a wheat-threshing machine which had been owned by a hot-rodding farmer. There was a reason for this. If they could be said to be fighting one thing, it was friction. Friction inside the engine generated heat in direct proportion to speed. Heat, in turn, caused engine parts to grow in size. Parts that would have fit tightly at highspeed, when they would be very hot, fit very loosely when the engine (or the transmission) wasn't hot.

The curves here were banked. Like Daytona, they were banked so steeply that cars had to move above a certain speed to avoid sliding off. Dave sat in the car jabbing the accelerator and waiting for the oil temperature gauge to move high enough so that he could get 60 miles an hour out of the engine without hurting it. He had to go at least 60 to avoid sliding off the turn.

As he waited, he found that he was nervously snapping and unsnapping and then snapping again the button at the wrist of his driving gloves. He tried to be angry with himself, for, after all, all he was about to do was go out on the track all by himself, and drive in leisurely circles. This didn't work. He knew that he was being critically examined, and that there was a very good chance that he would fail the examination.

The oil pressure gauge, up at 80 pounds per square inch, began to vibrate, and then to move slowly downward. The oil was becoming thinner as it became warmer. As if to prove this theory, the oil temperature gauge needle shook itself and began to move up the dial. Dave watched it, as his toe continued to tap the accelerator.

Then he shrugged his shoulders and squirmed in the seat. He pushed on the clutch, against 80 pounds of resistance, reached down with his right hand and shoved the rough-looking, smooth-as-glass shifting mechanism into low.

His toe tapped the accelerator again, and the roar of the engine rose in pitch. This time it didn't die down again, but grew heavier and more menacing. Dave let the clutch out as the ball of his foot pushed harder on the accelerator.

The tachometer began to wind upward. It dropped for a fraction of an instant as he went into second, and again as he went into high, and then it kept climbing. The engine, like a contented, giant leopard, emitted a deep-throated roar.

The suspension system began to pick up vibration from the cracks in the pavement and Dave stepped a hair heavier on the accelerator to break the sympathetic vibration. It was, in physical terms, a harmonic. He went around the first curve. From the tach at this speed (and there was no speedometer) he could only guess at his speed. But he was probably going 65 miles an hour. In this car, that was idling.

He picked up a little going down the straightaway, and entered the curve "on the rails," steering around the curve as anyone steers around a street corner. When he entered the first turn for the second time, he was doing 85 or 90, and he could feel the centrifugal force working on him.

As he went around a third time, making just about 100 miles an hour, he looked for the committee chairman. He saw him for a fraction of a second, long enough to see that he was making a winding motion with the index finger of his hand. Dave knew what that meant.

He shifted himself in the seat one more time as he entered the straightaway, and then, one hand at a time, without taking them from the tape-wrapped wheel, he flexed and stretched his fingers. Then he shoved his right foot as hard it would go to the floor. He felt a suggestion of fishtail as the full brute power of that incredibly powerful engine made its way to the wheels, but they didn't break loose. There was a suggestion of rising on its tail, but this too was a sensation, not a fact. The tachometer passed 4000 rpm. That was 100 mph on the nose. At 4400 rpm, or 110 mph, there were another few seconds of sympathetic or harmonic vibration, but this passed quickly. He felt, again, the centrifugal force pushing him down as he entered the far turn, and the force leaving him as the track flattened out. But he was not prepared for the force as he entered the near turn. He dropped his eyes for an instant to the tachometer, saw that it was nudging just beyond 5000 revs. His mind told him 125. He didn't see the committee chairman at all. He had been concentrating on the turn itself, and he looked at the tachometer. There hadn't been time.

The wind was screaming now, and the tires were howling and the noise of the exhaust, which had been loud enough to annoy him, was a dull rumble some place to his rear. Before he entered the far turn, he saw in a fraction of an instant that he was turning 5700 revs.

He was prepared for the tugging of centrifugal force on his body and on the steering, and for the accentuated feel of the road imperfections, magnified because the shocks were pressed down in their tubes, too, by the same force that worked on him.

He came out of the turn and held his foot to the floor. The tach needle kept crawling upward. 5500 again (he had lost 500 going into the turn), 5600. 5700. 5800. 5900. 5950. 6000. 6050. 6075.

Six thousand was 150 miles an hour.

All he saw of the committee chairman was a white blur.

Twice he saw the white blur. And the last time down the start-finish straightaway, the tach had hit 6300 revolutions per minute. He slowed now, not stepping on the brakes, which would have been useless at that speed, or even by taking his foot off the accelerator, but by gently easing the pressure of his foot on the accelerator. It is difficult to slow a racing car.

He was turning 3750 when he went into the near turn. The committee chairman was making another signal with his hands. It was a slow down sign. His hands made a pushing movement in front of his chest, and then his forefinger was drawn across his throat.

There was no mistaking the sign. Slow it down and cut it off. It took one more lap to slow it down gradually, so there would not be an unusual and damaging cooling in the engine and power train. Then he turned off the track.

The engine was noisy now, so noisy that he reached up and flipped off the toggle switch to the ignition, and then coasted the rest of the way in, to the relative quiet of squeaking, cooling metal.

The committee chairman was waiting for him in the pits. He didn't look happy, and Dave sensed that whatever the chairman was about to say, he didn't like his responsibility.

Dave got out of the car and pulled the helmet off and dried his sweaty face on a towel handed to him by Charley. Roger walked up and waited for the decision.

"You may or may not one day come to look on this as a favor, Wade," the chairman of the drivers' committe said, "but as much I would, frankly, like to, I can't find a reason to keep you off the track. You can handle the car, and you know what you're doing. You're cleared to race in the Grand National."

He put out his hand, and Dave shook it, but somehow it wasn't quite a celebration.

"Thank you," he said.

"You're welcome," the chairman said, and raised his hand in a little salute, and then walked away.

"Come on, Dave," Roger said. "I'll buy you some breakfast."

Fourteen

IT IS OFFICIALLY and for all time indelibly recorded that the entry of David Wade into Grand National Automobile Racing was something less than a rousing success.

He raced six times at Darlington. Four races of 100 miles, one race of 250 miles and one race for 400 miles. He did not place. He didn't even come close to placing. The highest he rose on the list of finishers was seventeenth, and that in one of the 100-mile races. Twice he didn't finish at all.

Once, he lost oil pressure and pulled into the pits. What had happened was that the oil-pressure-gauge line had failed. But the result was that he didn't finish the race. The second time he started and did not finish, he shifted down into second to avoid running into a bunch of cars ahead of him, and when he went back up into third, the transmission disintegrated. He found himself coasting to a stop in a blind rage, shifting into high and letting the clutch out and hearing the engine roar uselessly and without a load.

But for two days, the lap record at Darlington was held by Wade, D., 147.404 miles per hour. He lost the record to a Ford which turned 147.970.

In the qualifying race for the 400-mile race, Wade, D., had taken the fifth spot. That was as close as he'd been to winning, and that hadn't lasted one lap.

But there were no dents in the Fury. He hadn't bent it. And he hadn't torn up the transmission. There had been a whole series of improperly magnafluxed transmission gears that had slipped into the system. A whole series of gears that had failed as his had failed, leaving other men furious on the track as he had been.

But there were no consolation prizes. You either won or placed, or you did not win or place.

July turned into August, and Grand National racing headed South, to Daytona. The sports cars were gone. Off with the frolicking lambs and other sweet creatures, according to Roger, who placed sports cars and their amateur drivers in the same category as bird watchers and stamp collectors.

Roger and Charley rode down in the pizza wagon. Dave volunteered to take his turn behind the pizza wagon's wheel, but Roger pretended it was impossible for a racing driver to drive in straight lines.

"You're doing your share, Buddy. Really. Stop sweating."

He said this with so much sincerity that Dave didn't believe it. His share so far had been losing. He didn't like to consider how much money they were in the hole. He had a cold determination to win at Daytona. If that wouldn't make them rich, it would cut their losses. There were a large number of races at Daytona, and he felt that he should be able to win at least some of them.

But he didn't insist about driving. He had a stop to make on the way down to Daytona, a detour off Interstate 85 to Gainesville, in central Florida, home of the University of Florida.

He drove there, he looked at the bell tower, he watched the girls in summer school (and knew the girls watched, if not him, then the shiny Chrysler convertible), and exchanged stares with the official University alligator. He was told by a pleasant young man in the registrar's office that the University would be pleased to have him transfer as a junior, presuming that his transcript, once they wrote away for it, said that his grades were as good as he said they were.

What he thought of was that he would have to think of some good, solid, practical reason to transfer, a reason that would make good sense to his mother and stepfather when he called them on the telephone and made the announcement. So far, they had discussed very little during the weekly telephone calls except the behavior of the kids. He gathered that Comer had not felt it necessary to tell either his mother or Pete O'Hara that he had been a jailbird in Panama City. He thought that it didn't sound nearly as dangerous to be a racing loser as it did to be a racing winner. His mother probably thought all had been sweetness and cream. It was better that way.

He drove into Daytona Beach on U.S. 101, the oceanside

highway. He had been told that they were all going to meet at the Holiday Inn, and that the way to find the Holiday Inn was to stay on U.S. 101 and keep his eyes open.

But he followed, blindly, he thought, like the lemmings which blindly swim out to sea, a sign that said, TURN LEFT FOR DAYTONA INTERNATIONAL SPEED-WAY. He turned left, saw on a signpost that he was now on Volusia Boulevard, and kept going.

What he came to was a huge parking lot, and the rear of grandstands. A small, glass fronted building announced it-self as Track Headquarters. He pulled up in front, and went in. At a desk near the door sat a blue-eyed, blonde girl.

"Yes, sir?" she asked. She was young and tanned, and Dave smiled broadly.

"I'm Dave Wade," he said.

"Are you a driver, Mr. Wade?"

"Yes, I am. I wondered if my car and crew got here."

"Just a minute," she said, and she ran her fingers through a circular file.

"A Fury? Last run at Darlington?"

"Right."

"It's here," she said. "Came in early this morning."

"Do I need a badge or something to get into the pits?"

"Yes, sir," she said. "If you'll give me your license, please?"

It took a good ten minutes for her to fill out a thick stack of forms and tickets and badges.

"There you are, Mr. Wade," she said, and he thought it was perfectly delightful to have this tanned beauty call him

Mr. Wade. Then she said, "That'll be eighty-seven, seventy."

"Huh?" he said.

"Eight-seven, seventy. Dollars, I mean."

"Didn't Roger Chedister pick up the bill for this?"

"I don't have any record of it," she said.

"O.K.," he said.

When he paid her, it left him with $6.30.

In the car, before he started again, he went through the stack of tickets, documents, and passes. There was a pit pass, a paddock pass, an impounded area pass, a parking permit for his car, a second parking permit to be stuck on the windshield, a race meet drivers' license, and a stack of tickets, including tickets to the race dinner, scheduled, he saw, for that night, at the Princess Ilena Hotel.

That, he saw, accounted for $10.00 of the $87.70. He had two tickets for that, at $5.00 a ticket. Well, Roger would just have to cough up the money. This was a business expense. He wondered why Roger had failed to arrange things, and then decided he was acting like a prima donna. That was the right of a winning driver, but he hardly fell into that category.

Two huge storm sewer pipes, each large enough for a truck to drive through, ran under the track itself and into the paddock. There was an impatient blowing of horns behind him as he fumbled through the stack of credentials for his paddock pass.

"You'd save yourself some time, Buddy, if you stuck your sticker on the windshield."

"Sorry," Dave said.

There was another guard at a high fence separating the pit area from the paddock. He repeated his search for the right piece of paper for this guard. But finally he got inside. He got out of the car, went to a water fountain and soaked the decal in the refrigerated water. Then he mounted it triumphantly on the windshield: NASCAR DRIVER DAYTONA INTERNATIONAL SPEEDWAY PADDOCK AND PITS.

He walked the full length of the pits themselves, before he saw the familiar shape of the Fury and Charley's headless body bent over the engine. It was odd to think that he was really here, really at Daytona, really a certified, tested, approved (and officially equipped with $87.70 worth of credentials and dinner tickets) Grand National race driver.

"Hi, Charley," Dave said, and Charley came out from under the hood.

"Hi," he said.

"Got it running?" Dave asked.

"Yeah," Charley said, "it's running."

"Something wrong, Charley?" Dave asked.

"Have you seen Roger? Or Comer?"

"No. I came right here."

"Your mother is here," Charley said.

"My mother?"

"Your mother and your stepfather and the kids. And some other people. They came down from Marianna with Comer."

"Oh."

"You better go see them, huh?" Charley said.

"Is this running?"

"Yeah, but . . ."

"Charley, I've waited a long time to get a chance to drive a car like this at Daytona. I want to take it for a couple of laps."

"You don't have a license," Charley said.

"I just bought it," Dave said. "Why didn't Roger buy it, come to think of it?"

"You better ask him," Charley said, and then he smiled. "You take it around a couple of laps, Dave," he added. "Do you good."

He reached inside, tripped the toggle switch, started the engine.

"Let it warm up," he said. "I got a telephone call to make."

Dave put the racing coveralls on over his sport shirt and Bermuda shorts. He waited until the gauges showed the car was warm, and then he pulled out and onto the track. He had just shifted into second when an official furiously waved a black flag at him. He managed to stop before the end of the pit area, and he waited for the official to come up to him.

"What are you doing?"

"I was going to take a couple of laps," Dave said. "O.K.?"

"Who are you?"

"Wade."

"Oh, you own it, don't you. I've got a guy named Schellenberg down as the driver."

"I'd have a long talk with whoever gave you that list," Dave said. "I drive it."

"O.K.," the official said doubtfully. "You want to run against the clock?"

"Is it any trouble?"

"Not here it's not. We'll time every lap, and you just have to keep track of which lap is which."

"Fine," Dave said. "I appreciate that."

"Good luck," the official said. Dave let out the clutch and made a slow first lap around the Mecca for stock cars. He and everyone at Daytona would have agreed it was a slow lap, although the automatic timer printed: 81.008 on the roll of paper.

He took seven laps, each, with the exception of the last, faster than the one before: 109.655; 133.008; 145.308; 161.444; 163.563; 161.780.

He pulled into the pits, tired but elated, and when he saw his time, he was delighted with himself and with the Fury. He was going to take something here. He might not take the main event, but he was going to place in it, and he was going to take some of the lesser races. The Fury was running perfectly.

"Hey, Wade," the official who had black-flagged him off the course earlier said, and he wasn't friendly.

"Yeah?"

"I checked. The driver listed in the office for this car is Schellenberg. Louis Schellenberg. He's the guy that tore up the Chrysler at Winston-Salem last week. The office has got him listed as owner-driver."

"Well, there's something wrong."

"You said it," the official said. "And before you put that car on the track again, you get it straightened out."

"I will," Dave said. Roger was to blame. Roger was going to have to square this.

"I'm not kidding, Wade. We don't think stuff like this is funny down here."

"I'm not trying to be funny," Dave said.

He had the feeling that he was wrong, but he didn't know why.

And he couldn't find Charley when he walked back to the pits.

He was somewhat angry when he got into the Chrysler and drove away from the track and back toward U.S. 101 and the still unfound Holiday Inn.

He was not made much more cheerful when, as he stalked from the lobby of the motel to the room number he had been given, he saw, tanned and blonde and behind sun glasses, the unmistakable blonde hair and tanned skin of Anne Wagner. If Anne Wagner was here, so was old Rufus. That was all he needed to make his day complete.

He rapped on the door with a chrome-plated bolt he had been carrying about without quite knowing why for some time.

"Well, here he is, the Barney Oldfield of the Deep South," Pete O'Hara said, opening the door, putting out his hand, his warm smile instantly destroying Dave's anger. "And despite what your mother has led me to believe, you look positively healthy, and even prosperous."

"Hello, Pete," he said, and they shook hands.

The kids beat their mother to him, embarrassed to kiss him, demonstrating their affection instead by kicking him on the shins and pulling his hair.

It wasn't until after he had kissed his mother and disentangled himself from the kids that he saw Mrs. Wagner in a far corner of the room.

"Hello, Mrs. Wagner," he said.

"He's surprised to see me," she said. "I thought you'd see Anne downstairs."

"No, ma'am," he said.

"He even sounds like a southerner," Pete O'Hara said.

"He is half a southerner, you old Yankee you," his mother said, and then she turned to Dave. "Comer tells me that you want to go to the University with Anne next year, Dave."

That wasn't exactly what he had in mind. He wanted to go to the University, period. Or to go to the University so that he could race on weekends. Anne had nothing whatever to do with that. When he thought about it, though, the idea of Anne being there, if Rufus could be conveniently drowned or runover by a truck or something, had a certain appeal to it.

"Yes, ma'am," he said.

"Pete thinks it's a good idea," his mother said. "But I don't want you to do it just because of that."

"No, ma'am," he said.

"Watch yourself, Dave," Pete said, "Helen Wagner is the first mother of a female of our mutual acquaintance who approves of you."

"That's not true," Dave's mother said, loyally. "Not at all."

"Well, I do approve of him," Mrs. Wagner said. "Just to keep the record straight."

"You see, I told you," Pete O'Hara said, and then laughed. At that moment, without knocking, Comer came into the room, followed by Roger. He looked at Dave. "I want to talk to you," he said.

"I want to talk to him," Dave began. "I was practically accused of stealing the Fury and almost thrown off the track, and I want . . ."

"Dave, we sold the Fury," Comer said, flatly.

"What?"

"Say 'I beg your pardon,' dear," his mother said, "not 'what.' "

"I beg your pardon." Dave repeated dutifully.

"Don't blame him," Roger said. "I sold it."

"Would you mind telling me why?" Dave asked, and the sarcasm was thick and biting.

"I got a good price for it," Roger said. "Enough to make up our losses, and to buy another car. I sold it to Lou Schellenberg. He bent his totally at Winston-Salem."

"So?"

"So he has a chance to take this meet," Roger said. "And you don't, Dave, at least not this year. Next year, maybe."

"O.K.," Dave said. It was all he could trust himself to say. He got as far as the door.

"Dave . . ." Comer began.

"Let him go, Comer," Pete O'Hara said, and he said it

flatly, making it almost an order.

He didn't know where he was going. But he was going somewhere. He stalked back across the swimming pool, not even paying attention to Anne, in her tanned skin and blonde hair, the attention an object like that deserved.

He got behind the wheel of the Chrysler and found that he was shaking with rage. They had sold the car right out from under him, without telling him a word about it. They had no right.

"Are you going some place," Anne asked. "Or are you trying to twist the steering wheel off right here?"

"I'm going some place," he said.

"Then you better let me drive," she said. "I read in a magazine some place that people should not drive when they're angry. And you, Dave, are more than a little piqued."

Any other time, he thought, I would laugh at her and myself. But he slid over, and she got behind the wheel and started the car, backing it out as if she'd been driving it all her life.

"I haven't seen the speedway," she said. "So I think we'll go there."

"What if I don't want to go to the speedway?" he asked harshly.

"You don't have much to say about it, do you?"

"I don't have much to say about anything around here, apparently," he said.

She chuckled but didn't answer.

With the NASCAR driver sticker on the windshield they were waved past the guard. Anne drove all the way across the paddock, and put the nose of the Chrysler against the fence separating the paddock from the track itself. She pulled on the emergency brake, took off her seat belt, and curled her feet under her.

And then she began to talk about the University of Florida, about the faculty and the student hang-outs, about the customs and the rules. And he listened, and had just grown aware that she had calmed his anger, when she turned to him and asked, "What are you really mad about, anyway? How many juniors do you think will be at the University who've paid their own way as racing drivers? Do you always behave like a petulant little boy?"

"Frequently," he said, angrily, and then for some reason it was funny. "But there is generally some kind soul around, like Rufus, to knock me on my taillights before I get out of hand."

"Rufus is not a kind soul," Anne said, and she made this a statement of cold, unpleasant fact that told him that whatever competition Rufus might possibly be in the future, he would not be in the running for Anne.

He looked at her and smiled.

"I am in possession of a set of five dollar tickets to a dinner tonight," he said. "How would you like to go with me? As sort of my keeper?"

"I would like very much to go with you," she said. "But I'll have to ask my mother."

"Let's go ask her," Dave said.

"O.K.," she said. "Can I drive? It's not every day a lowly sophomore female gets a chance to drive a junior male transfer student around."

"Try to stay on the black stuff between the trees," he said.

A white Ford roared into the curve, tires screaming, exhaust an angry tatoo on a huge anvil.

"How fast was he going?" Anne asked, suddenly serious.

"He wasn't flat out," Dave said. "Hundred and fifty probably."

"How fast did you go?"

"One sixty three point five sixty three," Dave said, thoughtfully. She seemed to understand.

"You'll be back, Dave," she said. "There's lots of time."

"Yes, there is," he said; and he thought, there's lots of time for racing and for a great many other things.

"Let's go see if your mother will let you have dinner with me," he said, and he slumped down in the seat, and rested his head against the upholstery. He added, "Home, James."

"Put your seat belt on," Anne said. "Haven't you ever ridden in a car before?"